HOMELESS

MW01250583

EDWARD ALESSI

outskirts
press

1

HOMELESS

The church was quickly filled with well-dressed people and smiling faces. Aunts, uncles, cousins, neighbors and friends packed the church's pews in anticipation of the wedding. White and blue flowers graced the alter and the entrance to the pews held colorful bouquets. Everyone was excitedly waiting for the bride to walk down the aisle except that the groom was nowhere to be seen. Where was the groom?

A silence fell over the congregation as the organist played the traditional music, Here Comes the Bride and her father was about to make the traditional walk down the middle of the isle. The father of the bride stood tall with pride anxiously waiting to give his beautiful daughter away to the man of her dreams.

Suddenly, a black truck came crashing through the front door of the church, mowing down the bride, her father and the wedding party. Wooden door pieces, glass and metal flew into the air landing on the congregation who screamed at the horrific scene. The bride laid dead on the floor with blood splattering her white wedding gown.

As I struggled to catch my breath, breathing heavily like an Olympic runner who had just crossed the finish line, I was awoken from my nightmare by Mac, a 63-year-old alcoholic, who was vigorously shaking my shoulders. He was my roommate in this place we call the factory where I was a resident since March.

The place the homeless of Boston call home, the factory ,was an abandoned shoe factory. Over five years ago, it was a thriving and successful shoe factory that provided work for over 500 hundred workers. A two-level brick building which once stood proudly but now showed evidence of a decaying and deteriorating building with its broken glass windows that were boarded up with pieces of wood and crumbling red bricks. The dilapidated building now mirrored the people who currently lived in it. The building, like its occupants shared the same faith, that is being homeless. The company had abandoned the factory when it went into bankruptcy some four years ago. It now had become the unauthorized shelter for men like myself. This once, beautifully pristine building is currently surrounded by overgrown weeds which had replaced a perfectly manicured grassa. The parking lot did not escape the years of neglect as evidenced by the broken blacktop with weeds pushing their way up through the asphalt and debris strewn over its surface.

A chain linked fence surrounds the property with a sign saying KEEP OUT PRIVATE PROPERTY TRESPASSES WILL BE PROSECUTED. A sign that its new residents ignored. An opening was cut through the backend of fence which allowed people easy access to the building.

I along, with my new friends, found one of the offices, on the second floor which we claimed as our residence. The once colorful blue paint on the walls was now peeling. The door to the office was falling off its hinges. And broken furniture was strewn over the floor which was covered empty beer cans, food wrappers and broken wine. Each of the homeless in the building proudly protected their territory.

The guys at the factory were very territorial when it came to their space. Nobody dared to invade another man's claimed area without permission. At night, I would leave the factory to enjoy a warm supper and a comfortable bed at the Homeless Shelter.

In the morning the shelter would provide us with a nourishing breakfast but the Shelter had its rules. No drinking or drugs allowed. Fighting would get you ejected from the facility. Lastly, you were not allowed in the shelter during the day. Thus, I would spend much of the day pan-handling for money and hanging out with my new friends at the factory. That was our routine. The begging for coins would provide us with enough money to buy booze since many of us didn't' have any kind of income.

When you entered the front of the factory, you were greeted by broken hand rails that were clinging for life since they had lost their ability to support people. The concrete steps were sadly crumbling. The huge oak door that once welcomed people had two by four planks that attempted to keep people out but the men removed them. The first floor had housed the factories' machines. Now the machines laid silence with a blanket of rust that covered them. The machines rested motionless like bodies in a coffin with no life.

Periodically, the police would check-out the building and ask the homeless to leave but most of the time they ignored the men who occupied it. Questions that are frequently asked about the homeless are, who are they and how did they become homeless? Many of the men I had met were productive and responsible members of society but major life events have caused them to drink or use drugs and lose hope.

Was I one of those men? Yes. I once was married, had a beautiful family, and taught Social Studies at a local school. I was living my dream that eventually came crashing down all around me. The death of a child, unrelenting guilt, and alcohol lead to my leaving home. I took an apartment in Boston by myself and continued to drink until I lost my teaching job. My life eventually spiraled downward to being homeless. I was later evicted from my apartment because of non-payment I put all my belongings into a trash bag and found my way to the factory where I joined the rest of the homeless men, who had loss hope.

2

THE NIGHTMARE

I awoke from my nightmare screaming with fear, from my bed, which was made of carboard and an assemble of rags for a pillow and a discarded blanket. My whole terrified body was set in motion by the tremors that ripped through my person. Tears filled my eyes at the vision of this chilling sight. My nightmare abruptly came to an end by a comforting hand and caring voice, from my dear friend and companion, Mac, who yelled.

"Professor. Professor. It's me, Mac. You're having that nightmare again. Come on wake up."

My real name is Gregory Byrne. I acquired the name of Professor when I told the other homeless guys, that I was a middle school Social Studies teacher.

Mac tried to comfort me by putting his hand on my shoulder, and gently patting me on the back. "I don't have any answers as to your nightmares. I only know Professor, that you need help."

"These nightmares are all so real to me Mac. The worst part about them is when I looked into the truck, I see myself behind the wheel. It was me," I screamed.

"That's what really terrifies me. I'm the groom wearing a tuxedo. My wife is the bride and I killed her with my truck."

Mac took a dirtied bottle of whiskey from his torn and tattered jacket and said. "Here Professor, take a belt, it will help settled you down."

I happily accommodated him. "Sure. I need it."

With my hands still trembling, I greedily took a sip of the whiskey which brought me some relief as it trickled down my throat.

"Now doesn't that make you feel better Professor? Feel a little better?"

"Yes. Thank you, Mac. You're always there for me. Thanks."

My yelling and screaming soon brought the attention of my other comrade Larry, an 18-year-old homeless man, who shared the space with us. The three of us had forged an unbreakable bond. A bond that we all needed in order to survive in this uncaring world of throw-away humans. There wasn't anything we would not do for each other. We had each left our former families to form a new family.

We were one of many homeless men and women, who found themselves in this old abandoned factory that was waiting for demolition. Mac, Larry and myself were fortunate to find what looked to be one of the supervisor's office which had the remains of an old desk, and a few office chairs. The smell of urine, feces and decaying food were some of the smells that accosted the tenderness of your nose as you entered the building with its broken lock which was once used to keep out trespasses. The police along with the owners abandoned the security of the building for the past two years. This was my new home. A far cry from the beautiful house I once occupied in a quiet suburban neighborhood.

We were also very fortunate to find one of the rooms that offered us a degree of privacy but the room's door didn't have a lock.

Larry's dirty bearded face was filled with worry. I had become the father he never knew. Larry had left home when he was 16 years old. A home that had no father and an alcoholic mother who was prostitute. Larry said. "O, my God. You okay Professor? What happened? What's going on?"

Before I could answer, Mac spoke and calmed down our friend down.

"Larry. Everything is cool. The professor just had one of his nightmares, a bad dream."

Larry again, became irritated when he heard about my dreams. He repeatedly been hearing about them since he first met me. Larry got up from where he was siting and began to yell. "Dam it Professor. How many times have we told you to get help? How many times?"

I just threw up my hands saying. "I know you're' right but..."

Mac interrupted me before I could finish my sentence. "Shit Professor, no buts about it. Larry is right. What's the deal? Why don't you just go see Mary, the social worker at the Shelter?"

Larry than joined in the conversation. With a bit of sarcasm in his tone, he said. "What's the matter Professor? Afraid what you might find out about yourself."

I quickly discarded the old blanket that I was sitting on and started charging at Larry like a raging bull. "You son of a bitch, Larry. You don't know anything about me. Nothing."

Mac stopped me before I could throw a punch at him. "Settle down Professor. He didn't mean any harm. Listen, we just want to see you get the help you need. We care about you. We really do. We're your friends."

I soon backed away and my anger subsided. My feelings of fear and horror had turned to rage. I became angry because Larry was right. I didn't want to find out about myself. What was going on in my crazy head? Why had I decided to live this shitty life living in squalor? Maybe I deserved it. Maybe I just wanted to bury my painful past. I certainly didn't want some hot-shot social worker messing with my head, digging up memories. Memories I worked had worked so hard to bury.

I sighed and shook my head. "I'm sorry guys. I'm just not feeling myself. Larry, I didn't mean to go off on you. Maybe you're right. Maybe that's what got me so angry?"

Mac again asked me. "So, you going to see Mary today? If you want, we can go with you?"

Mary Cunningham was a young social worker in her twenties at the Pine Street Inn, a homeless shelter in Boston.

Larry with a smile on his face said. "We can all go Professor. He jokingly said. "We can call it your coming out party."

I couldn't help but laugh at Larry. There was a nugget of truth in what he said. It could very well be my coming out party. A time to realize what I am and who I am. I said. "Okay. Okay. You got me. I'll go today. Thanks for your encouragement. I really mean it, I'll go."

Larry looked at his watch. "You better go now. Mary will still be working at the shelter. It's 4:00pm. She'll be happy to see you."

"Let me get my gear and we can leave. You guys coming for supper at the shelter tonight?"

"I'll be there for sure." Said Larry.

I then turned to Mac "What about you Mac? Are you coming?"

"Not tonight. I might go over the Chinatown. I have a craving for some Chinese food."

We all laughed. Mac liked to go food picking in the dumpsters behind the restaurants. He seldom ate at the Pine street Inn.

"And what about tonight? I hope you're not going to sleep outside? The temperature is supposed to drop to 35 degrees." I said.

"I've got my sleeping bag. I'm good."

I shook my head. "You're always yelling about me getting help. You should take some of your own advice. You need to take better care of yourself Mac. You don't know what's in all that garbage you eat."

Mac gave a deep cough and just laughed. "I'll take my chances. I've done pretty good up to know."

This past month, I noticed that Mac's coughing had increased. I was becoming more concerned about his health.

Larry and I left the factory and headed to The shelter which was called Pine street Inn. It was a cool September day with the temperature barely reaching 51 degrees. A cool wind brushed our heads, which caused me to shiver. The site of the Inn brought a warm and comforting feeling. I wasn't looking forward to talking to Mary, this social worker. Mary Cunningham was a licensed social worker, who spent many an hour at the Inn. She was a very bright and beautiful woman. I could never figure out why she would want to work with a bunch of losers like us. Why she wasn't married with a house full of kids. Why she didn't seem to have a boyfriend. It just didn't figure. I thought to myself, *What a waste of a good woman.*

Once inside the building my heart began to race and my sweat drenched my hands like I had placed them in a bucket of water in spite of the weather. Did I really want to do this therapy shit?

3

THE VISIT

My dirtied, and unshaven face along with my tired body which was covered with filth and the faint smell of urine, walked into the Inn, the homeless shelter. In many ways, I really didn't care whether I lived or died. If I wasn't such a coward, I probably would have taken my own life but I didn't have the courage to do it. I was a real, all-around screw-up.

I suddenly began to think about my brother Frank and wondered how he was doing. How he and his wife Maria were doing. And their adopted son Danny. I also began to think about my wife Joan. My beautiful caring wife. Talk about screw-up? That was me. We had the perfect marriage, until. And my sweet daughter Alison. I bet all the boys are pursuing her. And my son.... My son. Wow.

My reverie was broken when Larry said to me, "Now remember Professor, you're going to see Mary. Make sure you do. I'll be waiting for you in the dining room and save you a set. We can enjoy a meal together."

I was now becoming irritated with Larry' constant

pushing me to get help. What the hell did he know about my life? He was just a kid. 18 years old. "Stop bugging me Larry. I said I'd go."

Larry put up his hands in defense. "Okay Professor. Won't say another word."

I proceeded to walk through the row of shelter offices that lined the far end of the room. When I reached the office that read, Mary Cunningham, social services, I stopped and stared at the name plate. It was like I had fallen into a trance. I again thought to myself, *do I really want to do this?*

After a few minutes, I knocked on her door, that opened and a soft quiet voice said, "Professor? What a surprise. Come in. Come in. I've been hoping that you'd show up one of these days."

I was puzzled by her comments. "What do you mean, you were waiting for me to show up?"

"Some of your friends have been talking about you. They're concerned. They felt you needed someone to talk to."

I threw my hands up in disgust. "They're a bunch of nosey bastards. They should mind their own business."

"Maybe. But I'd call them very good friends."

I took a deep breath and slowly but reluctantly moved into her office. What a contrast between the two of us. This pretty young women neatly dressed in a sweater and plaid skirt and me with my tattered clothing smelling like a garbage heap.

I took a seat in the chair closest to the door. Maybe, I was anticipating a quick exit.

On her desk was a folder with my name on it. She opened the folder and said. "I see you've been coming to the shelter for about three years. Is that correct?"

I looked down at the floor as she asked the question, feeling embarrassed and not wanting to make eye contact. "I guess so. I don't know. Whatever the record shows."

"They call you professor, but I know you have a name. Would you mind telling me what it is?"

I abruptly replied. "Gregory. Gregory Byrne."

"Well nice to meet you Mr. Byrne. Could you tell me what finally brought you to my office after all these years?"

"I guess it was the nightmares and the constant nagging by me friends."

"Nightmares?"

"Yes, nightmares. I keep having the same nightmare. Not all the time but when they happen." I took a breath. "They are very upsetting. I just can't take them anymore. I just can't."

"Could you tell me about them?"

I was getting angry by her continuous prodding and I clearly showed it. "Why? What good will it do? They're nightmares. What can you do about them?"

"Maybe, working together, by talking about them and your problems will help."

"What do you mean working together? I don't know anything about all that shit. You talk. I'll listen."

"I might be the social worker but we can only solve what's bothering you, by both of us working on your problem together."

I shook my head and replied "I guess so. I don't know."

"Why don't you start by telling me about your nightmares"

I than related the horror of my nightmares to her. "So, what do you think doc?"

"To begin with, I'm not a doctor. I am a trained social worker. I'd like to know what you think they're about?"

I now became angry with her. "How the hell should I know? I keep telling you. I'm not a social worker. That's your job."

"I gather you're not ready to talk about them ."

"You have that right lady. I don't want to talk about them. Let me ask you a few questions."

"I guess that's fair."

"What the hell are you doing in a place like this and why aren't you married, at home with a bunch of kids? You shouldn't be associating with all these drunks and addicts."

"To begin with, I'm here because I want to be. I like helping men like yourself.

"These men are not just drunks and addicts but human beings who are currently having some real problems. You asked about my not being married? I do have a boyfriend. Maybe marriage is in the future."

Anger began to fill my voice. "You know lady you shouldn't even be here. You don't know a dam thing about what us guys are going through." My anger turned to sarcasm. "I can just picture who you are. Rich girl living in a fancy house. Two nice parents to take care of you. Give you anything you want. Never really had to work for anything. Never really knew what suffering and pain was all about."

I just started to get up out of chair and walk out of her office when she returned my angry. She quickly responded, to my characterization of her. "Mr. Byrne, you come right back here and sit down. You think you know me but you don't know a dam thing about me. When

I was eight, my parents split. My mother was cheating on him. I was raised by my dad but almost never saw my mother again. She was far from the perfect mother. When I was seventeen, my father contracted pancreatic cancer. I was devastated. Completely devastated. I didn't come from an ideal family. Don't give me that bullshit about how I don't know pain. How I don't know suffering. But there're differences between you and me. I didn't stop living and feeling sorry for myself. I did something with my life. I didn't drown my troubles in a bottle of booze."

I became speechless and taken aback by her story. I wasn't expecting that kind of a response from her. Wow. What a firecracker. A spark. Mary was almost in tears as she related her story. I then felt like an ass. A real dope.

Mary then quickly gained her composure and apologized to me. "I'm sorry Mr. Byrne. That was unprofessional. I don't know what to say."

"No. No. I'm the one who should apologize. I feel like a real dope."

"Okay. Let's start all over again."

I sighed and said. "Sounds good to me."

"Let me begin by telling you about someone who may be able to relieve your nightmares. Dr. Wilburn comes here once a week. I think he can prescribe some medication that will help with the nightmares. But that's only one part of the treatment plan for you. Secondly, you need to talk. No matter how painful, you need to talk to me Mr. Byrne. Do you understand me?"

"What is he, a shrink? So, you probably think I'm crazy?"

Mary sat back and laughed. "Yes, he is a Psychiatrist

but you're not crazy. He should be back here next week. Monday is his day to visit. What do you say? Medication can give you some relief from those terrible nightmares."

"I'll give it a try."

"Good. Why don't we call it quits for today? How about seeing me next week? Will that work for you?"

I broke into an uncontrollable laughter. "I don't know Mary. I'll have to check my appointment book."

My remarks caused Mary to laugh. "I'm sorry....."

I interrupted her attempt to explain why she asked if the appointment was good for me. "Forget it."

After leaving Mary, I was feeling pretty good about my visit. It went much better than I had anticipated. As I left her office, I knew my friends were going to pepper me with a hundred questions. But I was ready for them.

4

LARRY'S STORY

While I was in Mary's office, I couldn't help but feeling like I had rejoined the human race. My brief little talk with her, who wasn't a homeless or a drunk, made me feel like a person again. But once I stepped out of her office door and into the dining room, the reality of being homeless hit me in the face like a bucket of cold that was tossed over my head. *So, I thought to myself, maybe seeing Mary might turn out to be a good thing. And maybe that doctor could help me with my nightmares.* For the first time in a very long time, I had hope which had eluded me over the past three years.

When I returned to the table, Larry, got up and said. "So, what she like? What happened?"

I had one shit-eating grin on my face, when I saw him. "Slow it down Larry. Give me a chance to catch my breath. Let me start by saying she's one hell of a woman. Not only is she a kind and caring person but someone you don't want to mess with. I liked her. As a matter of fact, I'll be seeing her every week."

And Larry, anxiously asked about my nightmares. "And what about your Nightmares? What did she say about them?"

"That's another piece of good news. She referred me to the doctor, who comes here once a week who could give me some medication to deal with them but Mary made it very clear, I needed to talk, spill the beans."

Larry patted me on the back saying. "Hey, that's great Professor. I'm so happy for you. Glad things worked out."

"I need to thank you and Mac for all your encouragement. If it wasn't for you two, I wouldn't have gone for help."

"Hey what are friends for?"

I suddenly came to realize that these people were truly my good friends. Whether it was to share a bottle of cheap wine or a discarded blanket to keep out the cold or a fire in an oil drum to keep us warm.

They, like me, had turned to a homeless life, to escape from the unpleasant realities of their own lives and to become invisible to the world.

But Larry was a person I really felt sorry for. He was a young man of 18 years, with his whole life in front of him and yet his life was over. One day when we were sharing a bottle of wine, he told me his story, a sad story.

Larry was the victim of a horrible and unthinkable family, if you want to call his home a family. His life began as an unwanted pregnancy. His mother had started her life as a prostitute at the age of 15. She never took the necessary precautions to prevent a pregnancy until she had Larry at the age of 16. She should have given him up for adoption but decided to keep him. Larry never knew his father nor did his mother.

His mother, Maggie also came from a very dysfunctional family. She fled from an intolerable home life consisting of an abusive alcoholic father and a prostitute mother. So, the familial cycle continued to produce emotional turmoil and maladaptive humans.

His mother, became a street walker, which is the lowest status in the hierarchy of prostitutes. She was dominated by her pimp, who abused her. He called himself Mr. B. She would frequently conduct her business in her small three-room apartment, in the poorer section of Boston. Many a night he could hear the moans and groans of her clients. No matter what he did, he couldn't block out those horrible sounds. There were also times when the Johns would beat her. His attempts to intervene and try to protect his mother would result in his getting beat up.

Now Prostitution wasn't her only problem. She would use alcohol to suppress her painful hopeless life. Larry, learned at a very early age, to deal with his problems thru the use of booze, just like his mother. One day he decided that he had enough of living with an alcohol prostitute of a mother. The depressed woman he called his mother. He thus packed his bags with his meager belongings and left home. He felt that anything would be better than his current life. He could no longer tolerate his mother being used and abused by this man called Mr. B. her pimp and at times his mother abusing Larry.

So, like his mother, he took to the streets of Boston at the tender age of 15 to become one of the many homeless teenagers.

About three months after leaving home, I found Larry, in a Boston side alley drunk, and beaten.

Someone had stolen his meager savings and left him there, to bleed to death. I quickly got some help from a policeman and he was taken to the Boston City Hospital where they cared for his injuries.

From that day on, we became the best of friends. In many ways, our relationship transcended our friendship to me becoming a father to him. I became the father he never knew. The father he so desperately wanted. I thought to myself. *What a joke. Me his father? I wasn't exactly the father of the year. I couldn't even be a proper father to my own children.*

The day I took him back to my place in the Factory, I looked into his face and desperately tried to contain my tears, since looking at him resurrected feeling about my own son, my son who no longer existed. Thus, Larry became a part of our Family, Mac and myself.

5

THE COUGH

A week had passed, and it was time for my second visit with Mary. Larry went ahead of me to supper at the Shelter while I was talking to Mac. Mac's cough had become more persistent over the past week, which caused me to become even more concerned about him. He also appeared more lethargic and seldom left the factory except to find some dumpster food. His ongoing smoking of discarded smoking material from cigars to cigarettes certainly didn't help his sickly condition.

I approached Mac who was sitting at the desk playing solitaire.

I began by saying. "How's it going old friend?"

"Not bad Professor. I think I'm finally going to win this time."

"That's good. Mac, I wanted to talk to you about your cough. It seems like it's getting worse."

"No. Same old thing. Probably a little cold or due to my smoking. I need to cut back on the weeds, that's all. Will you look at that? Four more cards and I've made it."

"Mac, will you at least consider seeing the Doc at the Shelter?"

"Sure Professor. I'll give it some thought. Now go along before you miss your appointment with Miss Mary." Jokingly he continued. "I've never met her but Larry said she's hot. No wonder you don't mind seeing her."

I couldn't help but laugh. "Mac, you are something. See you when I get back."

"Have a good meal."

I arrived at the Shelter and looked around for Larry when a voice said "Over here Professor. I saved you a seat."

"Thanks Larry. Appreciate you saving me a spot. I want to ask you something, if you don't mind?"

"Sure, whatever you want. Shoot."

"I think Mac is getting sicker, I mean real sick. He needs help. Some real medical attention for his cough. Haven't you noticed how he's coughing more and his coughs are deep. He's spending more time at the factory. He doesn't even go out with us anymore."

Larry than turned to me. "Now that you mention it, yes I do. But he always had a cough. Ever since I've known him. I just don't think much about it."

"I know but now it's worse, much worse."

Larry said "I'm not surprised, with all that shit he eats out of the restaurant dumpsters."

"Let's keep pushing him to get help. Okay?"

"You have it Professor?"

"By the way, what's for chow tonight Larry?"

With a broad smile on his face Larry said. "Meatloaf. Cookie is on tonight. How about that?"

My eyes lit up like lights on a Christmas tree. "Meatloaf. Great."

Cookie, was an excellent and professional cook, who volunteered his services once a month. He made very simple basic foods but they were extraordinary. The best. He worked at one of the up-scale Boston restaurants but made the finest meatloaf in the world. I always looked forward to his suppers.

"All right Larry, let me go see Mary. I'll be back before dinner is served."

"I'll be here. He laughed. "I don't have any important dates this evening."

I got up from the table took a deep breath and went to Mary's office.

In spite of the cold, I found that my hands had become sweaty at the thoughts of a second meeting. I knew this time our conversation wouldn't be so casual. She would probably be digging into my past.

6

ANOTHER VISIT
TO THE SOCIAL WORKER

I went to the office a few minutes earlier for my visit. When I knocked on the door, Mary said." Give me a few minutes Professor, I'm just finishing up with a client."

"Okay. I'll be right outside."

I took a seat on the wooden bench that was right outside her office. I was still preoccupied with Mac's condition. I was hoping that he would get help but wasn't very confident that he would do anything about his condition.

Ten minutes passed before a young man exited the office. I had seen him before. He was an Ex-Marine who was struggling with drug addiction.

Mary soon came to the door and said, "You can come in Professor. I'm ready."

I thought to myself, *you're ready but I'm not.*

"Have a seat Professor. I was thinking, I know everyone calls you Professor but would you mind if I call you Mr. Byrne?"

I replied nonchalantly, "Whatever makes you happy Mary."

Mary immediately picked up on my preoccupation.

"Looks like you have something on your mind?"

"I do. My good friend Mac. His cough is getting worse. I'm trying to get him some help."

"That's so good of you. Maybe I can help with that."

"That would be great. I would very much appreciate it."

"Now, let's get back to you. Why don't you start by telling me a little bit about yourself? Maybe begin with your family and what it was like growing up. Okay?"

I took the deep breath and began. "To start with, there's only my brother Frank and myself. He's older than me by 7 years. Always been a part of my life. Great guy."

"No other family."

I hesitated for a moment. Not knowing if I wanted to talk about my other family members.

Mary persisted. "Mr. Byrne? Did you hear what I said? Do you have any other family members?"

"I took another deep breath and said. "I do. A daughter and a s..." I started to say son and corrected myself. "I'm separated from my wife."

"A daughter. How nice. How old is she?"

"Now." I thought for a minute. "Now, she must be about 16 years old. I think"

"You must miss her?"

I again hesitated for a few seconds. "I would love to see my little girl. She was only 12 years old when I left home. For now, let's leave it, at that."

"Okay Mr. Byrne. And what about your wife?"

"I don't think I'm ready to talk about her either, if that's okay with you."

"Whenever you're ready. Anyone else?"

"Yes, my mom, or I should say my adopted mom."

"What do you mean, an adopted mom? Did she adopt you and your brother Frank?"

I laughed. "No. We adopted her but that's a long story. We'll get to her later."

"It seems like you don't want to talk about a lot of things. Is there anything you can talk about? What about your brother Frank? Have you seen or heard from him since leaving home?"

I abruptly said. "No contact."

"You seem to be very evasive Mr. Byrne."

"I guess I am but talking about myself is not easy for me. I'm not use to letting people know about life."

"Maybe you can start by telling me something about your parents and growing up in your own family."

"It's been a long time."

Mary was always very patient with me. Never pushing too hard, but at times, giving me a gently push to talk. "Okay Mr. Byrne. We need to start somewhere if I'm going to help you. Begin somewhere. Just tell me what you can."

I cleared my throat. "Well, life was just okay until I was about five years of old. Like I said, it was just Frank and myself. Frank, was always there for me. Nobody in school would give me a hard time because of him. I was a very shy quiet boy compared to Frank. He was much more outgoing."

"So, he was your protector. Always there when you needed him?"

"Always. Even when I got older. If I needed advice or money, Frank gave it to me."

"And what about your mother? Did you get along with her?"

"My mother? You mean the bitch? My mother."

I abruptly got up and left her office because the very thought of my mother was too upsetting. I hated my mother and she probably hated me. I left Mary's office. I know I shouldn't have left without an explanation but I just couldn't express my feelings about my mother since they were colored with rage. Besides, Mary was still a stranger to me. A nice person but still a stranger.

When I returned to the dining room to eat with Larry, he immediately knew something was wrong. My face was a bright red and my eyes were moist with tears trying to break through. "What the hell happened to you in there?"

"It wasn't good. Too much shit. I don't know if I made a mistake trying all this therapy. It just isn't working. Too dam painful."

Larry was very sympathetic and supportive of me. "I'm sorry to hear that Professor. What can I do for you? Anything?

".Just do what you're doing. Glad you're here"

"Will you be going back to see her?"

"I don't know. I don't think so."

"Think about it, Professor. Don't give up now. I know it's tough on you but this is what you need to do. Work things out. Get all that pent-up crap out of your system."

"I'll give it some thought Larry. Let's save some of this food for Mac. I don't think he's been going dumpster-diving for his dinner or eating anything."

"Good idea. Will do. Well' let's get in the line. At least you should be able to enjoy Cookie's meatloaf."

"Thanks for being there for me Larry."

"Hey, Professor. What are friends for?"

"When we get back to the factory tomorrow, don't let Mac know what happened tonight. Okay. He' doesn't need to worry about me."

"You have it Professor."

7

MAC'S STORY

The next morning, we ate breakfast at the shelter, and returned to the factory. It was a cold and wet day as we made our way home, to the factory. When we reached our place, we found Mac fast asleep in the room. We had brought some breakfast food along with some meatloaf and bread from last night's meal. I hated to wake him up but it was 10:00 in the morning.

I approached Mac and gently tapped him on the shoulder. "Hey mac, it's time to get up."

He slowly raised his head and said. "What? What? What's going on?"

"Time to eat. We brought you some breakfast and a bottle of water. There was no way I could get some coffee for you."

"Thanks guys. The water will do. Appreciate it."

He greedily chowed down all the food, not caring to save the meatloaf for another time. I could tell that he hadn't eaten for a few days.

In between chewing on his food, he said, "Wow this stuff is great."

"You should join us one of these days. There's more food like that at the shelter."

"Maybe I'll do that. Meant to ask you. How did things go with your sessions Professor?"

"Good. Went well." I didn't want to tell him that I had become so upset that I walked out of her office. As I spoke, I looked towards Larry as if to say don't mention a thing.

Larry then said, "I know it's kind of nasty out there but I think I'll go uptown and do a little pan-handling. We can use some money. Why don't you stay with Mac Professor?"

"Are you sure?"

"Definitely. I'll be back right after noon."

"Thanks Larry." As Larry left the building, Mac again began to cough.

"O, Mac. That cough doesn't sound good. Why don't you let me take you to see the Doc at the shelter?"

"Next week. I promise."

"Mac, we've known each other now for what? Two years."

"That's about right."

"But I don't know a thing about you."

Mac nonchalantly replied. "So, what's there to know?"

"Do you have a family? What kind of work did you do? How did you end up here, homeless?"

Mac laughed and continued to dodge my questions. "You sound like your social work friend, Mary. Asking all those questions. How I got here is a long story Professor. Not too interesting."

"Come on Mac, give me something."

Mac gave a big sigh and said. "Let's see, where do I begin?"

I thought about what Mary, my social worker, would say. "You can begin, wherever you like. Whatever is most comfortable for you." Here I was pushing Mac to tell me about himself and get him help and I walked out of Mary's office. What a hypocrite.

One thing I did know about Mac, he was a very intelligent, bright guy, quite different from many of the alcoholics and druggies around here. I couldn't help but wonder what went wrong in his life?

To begin with, you might wonder how he got the name Mac. It was a name given to him by the homeless community but his real name was Johnathan Macintyre. He was a man in his sixties, who clearly demonstrated the results of a past that was riddled with turmoil. He was a kind, considerate, honest and compassionate man and I do emphasize the word honest. Right is right and wrong is wrong. There was no in between. No gray areas. These wonderful traits, were probably the qualities that brought him to be homeless. Isn't that Ironic?

Mac started his story by saying. "Let me begin by saying, I was employed as a design engineer for an automobile firm. It was a very good paying job. Made myself a lot of money. And I had a wonderful family. Was married to a beautiful woman and was blessed with three beautiful daughters." Mac then stopped talking and removed a photograph from his coat and said. "These are my daughters and my wife."

"There beautiful Mac. Knockout gorgeous. And your wife, what an attractive woman."

He laughed. "How could my daughters not be attractive with a mother like her."

"I assume that they all went to college?"

"Yes, they all had attended Boston College and graduated with high honors. My wife went to Simmons in Northampton, Ma. She was a very bright star but one of the most caring people you'd ever want to meet. Her name was Margaret but we always called her Susan. She never liked the name Margaret so she used her middle name which was Susan."

When my daughters were born, Susan decided to be a stay at home mom. I told her that I was making enough money to hire a nannie. But she insisted on caring for the children, at least until they go to school. My wife wanted to be a grant writer for non-profit organization. That was Susan. Had no or little interest in money but like me, she wanted to make a difference in the lives of people."

"She sounds like quite a woman. Why would you give her and your family up? Your family sounds like the ideal family."

"Things happened Professor that are out of our control."

"I don't mean to pry but what do you mean?"

Mac suddenly became tearful. His head dropped into his lap. He slowly began to get the words out of his mouth.

"Cancer Professor. Cancer. She died of cancer, ovarian cancer. My daughters and I were devastated. Life seemed to stop. My world came to an end. She was the heart and soul of our family. That was the something that was out of my control."

"How old were your daughters when you wife passed?"

"Let me see, Katherine who is my oldest was in her first year of college, and Elizabeth was still in High School, a senior.

I felt bad for pushing Mac on the subject. "I'm so sorry Mac. I. I...." I began to stutter. The words got stuck in my dry.

"Professor. Don't worry about it. It's okay. It still hurts even thou it's been a while." He quickly gained his composure and continued his story. "I went to college, Tuft's University where I got an engineering degree and later got my Masters in Design Engineering. I loved engineering. It made you think. Be creative in solving problems.

I did my internship at a company that later hired me. I started working for them as a junior engineer and quickly progressed to a senior engineering position. As much as I loved the work, my family always came first. I have to admit it, to balance a demanding job with one's family was not easy job."

"I can't begin to imagine what it was like losing your wife, raising three children and going to work every day."

"Not easy, but somehow life goes on with or without you. I needed to tend to my daughters, so I decided to go on with my life.

Three years went, by following her death when we were blessed with a new happiness. My oldest daughter Katherine, had been seeing a guy she started to date in High School. She had a beautiful June wedding. I gained a son-in-law. A great guy. My other daughter, went to college and graduated with honors. I couldn't have been more proud of them. These were good times until a second tragedy in my life struck but not with my family."

"What happened?"

"A piece of auto equipment I designed malfunctioned

which resulted in the death of two people, who owned our vehicle. One of the victims was a 24-year-old college student and the second victim was an 80-year-old woman. I was devastated but I knew how to correct the problem. It would mean that the company would have to recall hundreds of cars, which would be costly. It was the kind of a problem that affected some cars but not all of them. I felt that the death of two people was two, too many. The company decided not to recall the vehicles since it would cost millions of dollars. They also believed that the possibility of the problem reoccurring was rare..

I argued and fought with them to recall the vehicles but they refused to do it. I couldn't have the death of future people on my conscience especially when there was a way to correct the problem. I went to every regulatory governmental agency to have them force the company to recall the vehicles but my efforts couldn't compete with the cadre of compony lawyers. Needless to say, I was fired. I started to drink and found that I couldn't sleep nights.

Between the loss of my wife and the guilt I carried about the equipment I designed, I didn't want to live anymore. Life was intolerable, so intolerable that I attempted suicide by taking a bottle of my wife's pills. I would have been dead if it were not for my younger daughter, who came home, found me and called 911. I ended up at the MacClane Psychiatric Hospital. I didn't want to be there and was overwhelmed with the shame I brought upon my family. I also didn't want to face my daughters for what I had done so I eloped. And here I am."

"But Mac, you did all you could do to deal with the

problem. Why carry the burden of guilt? It was the company's fault not yours.

"I gave up. I didn't do enough to fix the problem Professor. End of story."

As Mac related his story I couldn't help to think of my own family and why I was homeless. My story was not unlike his, filled with guilt.

8

MAC AGREES TO GET HELP

Thursday soon rolled around and it was time for my third visit to see the social worker, Mary Cunningham. I was anxious about seeing her, since I had walked out of her office and I didn't' want to talk about my past, a past I had spent years, trying to bury it deep within the recesses of my fragile mind and broken heart

The thought of seeing Mary again, prompted me to lose my patience with Mac. I and Larry have been frantically urging him to see a doctor about his cough but the stubborn bastard wouldn't budge on the matter. I refused to stand idle while one of my best friends was killing himself.

Just before we were getting ready to leave for supper at the shelter that Thursday, I said to Larry "Go ahead, I'll be there in a few minutes."

After he left, I went over to Mac and started yelling at him. "I don't get it Mac. What are you doing? You're killing yourself? I know you want to die but I'm not going to let you. You hear me old fool? You're not going to die."

Mac laughed. "Now you have it Professor. I want to die. I tried it once before but it didn't work. I screwed up. What the hell do I have to live for? The genius that I was supposed to be, messed up. Two innocent people are dead because of my mistake. Two innocent people. Don't you get it Professor?" Mac began to raise his voice and started yelling at me. "Are you that dense?" And how many more people will have to die because of me? Huh professor. How many more?"

"Come on Mac, you tried to fix that problem but the company wouldn't listen to you. They are the ones who should be carrying the guilt, not you. You said you could fix the problem but they wouldn't listen. Their greed will be responsible for any further deaths."

"But I was the one that created the malfunction to begin with. Just let me die Professor. Just let me."

"Your stubborn old selfish bastard. Open your eyes. Can't you see that I don't' want to lose another person in my life. You and Larry are all I have now. If you don't do it for yourself, do it for me. Do it for Larry."

Mac was stunned by what I said. He didn't know how to react to it. He just shook his head and said. "I don't know what to say professor. It's been a long time since anyone cared about me."

"Not really Mac. Not really. I bet your daughters care about you. Do they deserve to lose their father? They already lost their mother. I know they want you to live?"

"But they don't deserve a shit like me. They don't."

"Come on Mac, don't give me that. It was not intentional Mac. You did your best. You tried to correct the problem. You did your best"

"I know Professor, but I've had enough of life." Mac

than responded to my anger with anger. "Just let me die in peace. What the hell are you doing to me Professor. Just let me go. I tell you, I'm no good to anyone."

"I'm begging you Mac. Please. I'm begging you. Let us help you. Maybe you can see Mary, the Social worker and she can help you sort it all out."

A small smile suddenly appeared on Mac's face as he said. "Now that would be something. Me talking to a social worker. I don't know about that but I'll tell you this, to make you happy, I'll go with you to the clinic to see the doc, tomorrow. There. You happy now?".

I gave him a hug and said. "As a matter of fact, I am. Very happy." You know Professor, you're such a pain in the ass. Now, get the hell out of here and let me get some rest. You have an appointment with that cute little social worker. I know why you want to see her. If I was younger, I'd be chasing that skirt but not for counseling."

I left the factory, feeling good that that Mac had finally agreed to seeing the doctor tomorrow. As I left the room I said. "Listen. Don't go to any dumpsters tonight. I'll bring some good food back to you."

Half laughing Mac replied. "Gee Professor, don't you ever give up. Just get the he'll out of here."

I than joined my friends at the shelter and went to my appointment with Mary after telling Larry, that Mac agreed to see the Doc.

9

RETURN TO MARY

I decided to return to Mary and continue with my counseling. The word mother had brought up some intense feelings that extended beyond anger, they were feelings of hatred and rage. I know they say it's important to forgive but I could never forgive her for what she did to me and my father.

When I returned to Mary, she was still sitting behind her desk, with the door open, as if she knew I would return.

"Mr. Byrne, I'm so glad you came back. I can readily see that talking about your mother has brought up a lot of angry and unpleasant feelings."

"You'll never know. Maybe you're happy that I returned to see you but I'm not sure it's the same for me. One other thing?"

"What's that?"

"No more Mr. Byrne. Just call me Greg or Professor."

"Not a problem. If you wish. Can we continue your conversation about your mother?"

I reluctantly replied. "I guess so."

"Tell me about your mother. Why just the thought of her, evokes such anger?"

"That bitch. I'd love to."

She then repeated the word "bitch."

"You heard me. Bitch. That's what she was, a bitch. My mother was a very beautiful attractive woman. I can see why my father married her. She was also a very ambitious woman, who enjoyed status and wanted to make a name. All she cared about was herself. I never quite knew why she married my father, a builder, a construction worker except that he was developing a thriving business which meant money for her."

When I was born, I was a mistake. A mistake that interfered with her career, her precious career. My dear mother didn't want to have any more kids. She wasn't planning on having me according to my brother and father. I was an inconvenience. When she became pregnant, she was furious. She wanted to get an abortion, which angered my father. My father was a devoted Roman Catholic thus an abortion was definitely out of the question. He said she was going to have the baby whether she liked it or not. My dad always made sure that we got to church with him on Sundays, while she slept until noon."

"Did your mother practice any religion?"

I couldn't help but laugh. "Are you serious? The only God she worshiped was money and her career."

"But what did she do when your brother Frank was born?"

"When Frank was born, she returned to work once he was in school. He was 7 years old at the time of my birth."

In order to placate my mother, my dad hired a Nani

to take care of me and my brother so that she could continue her career. She hardly spent any time with me or my brother. Our Nani who was a wonderful person in her sixties, who became our mother."

"And what about your father?"

He was a different story. Dad always made as much time as he could for us. Even when he came home from working early in the morning until seven in the evening, he would do something with us. On his off days my dad, would take us to amusement park or to a ball-game or an ice cream."

"Well, didn't you mother go with you on these outings?"

"Almost never. A few times when we went to the beach, she would come to show off her perfect body. She liked wearing those skimpy bathing suits just to get a rise out of some of the men on the beach."

"So, your saying she was never a mother to you or Frank? She only cared about herself?"

"Not only not a mother but not a true wife to dad."

"What do you mean?"

"When it happened, it was no surprise to any of us. I think my father suspected it was coming. I don't think he wanted to admit it to himself."

"What was coming?"

"The bitch was fooling around with some guy she had been working with.

One evening there a was a huge fight between the two of them about her, having an affair. The arguing was fierce and vicious. I never heard my father get so angry. It ended with her packing her bags and leaving the house. Before long they were divorced. There was some kind of settlement with my father getting custody of us. She didn't contest my father being awarded full custody. As a matter of fact, she liked the idea. She finally got rid of us. From that time on we saw her a few times here and there but not very much."

"How did you feel about what happened?"

"That's a dumb question. I said good riddance. The bitch was out of our lives."

"And what about your father? How did he take the divorce?"

"He was heart-broken. He still loved her in spite of what she did to him. Can you believe that? After all she did, he still loved her."

"I guess there are some things that are hard to understand."

"You're right, I didn't get it. It was months before he came back to his old self. With her gone, we didn't miss her. My dad was always both mother and father to us."

"And how old were you when all of this took place?"

"I was six when the divorce was finalized."

"That's an awful lot for a young child to experience."

"Yes and no. In many ways I was happy that she was out of our life. I had my brother and father. I loved my dad. He was my everything."

"You used the past tense. Is he dead?"

I began to cry. I could no longer contain my tears. In between my tears I said. "He's dead." The room went silent. Mary didn't say a word except to comfort me and hand me a tissue

"Want to tell me about it?"

"I'm sorry. I got to go."

"I understand Greg. I'm so sorry. See you next week?

"Sure."

10

THE DEATH OF A FRIEND

My meeting with Mary resurrected a lot of feelings about my dad. It was too painful to talk about his passing. Right now, I just wanted to focus my attention on the living, my friend Mac.

The next morning, I woke up grabbed a quick breakfast at the shelter and was anxious to rush back to the factory. I got up from the table where Larry was still eating and chattering with some of the guys. When I got up he said. "Hey Professor, what's the big rush? We have no place to go."

"I have something I need to do. See you later."

I couldn't wait to see Mac and get him to the clinic. I was determined not to let him say no. Not this time. Even if I had to carry him on my back, he would be coming with me.

I don't know why I had become so attached to this guy, so obsessed about his welfare. Maybe he reminded me of my dad? I don't know. My head just seemed all messed up. Too much going on.

When Mary brought up my brother, I couldn't help

but wonder how he was doing. Was he still single or had he got married? I missed Frank along with my father. They were so much a part of my life. I missed them. I wondered what the hell I was doing spilling my guts to this broad. My meeting with Mary also triggered feelings about my daughter Alison. I wondered about her. Was she still playing soccer? Did she have a boyfriend? I really missed my family. Maybe leaving home was a mistake? I began to question my decision. Then I began to think that I didn't deserve them or any kind of happiness.

I just didn't know. All this counseling shit is stirring up a lot of things in my head. A lot of feelings. I even had some doubts about continuing with Mary.

I finally reached the factory building and entered through the side door, which was hanging off its hinges. We were not the only homeless people that called this depilated factory home. We had plenty of company.

When I found Mac, he was sleeping on the floor under a piece of cardboard. An old blanket was wrapped around him.

I thought to myself, *I hate to wake him up.*

I shook Mac's shoulders and said, "Come on Mac my friend, time to go to the clinic."

There was no response.

The next time, I shook him a little harder and he rolled over on to his back. His body was limp. Still no response. I started yelling and slapping him in the face. He didn't move. I checked his pulse. No pulse. Mac was dead. Dead.

I just stayed, kneeling beside my treasured friend. He was dead I kept saying it. My mind had troubling processing the reality of his death. Mac was dead.

Gone. He finally got what he wanted. He had completely lost his will to live. Dead. Tears began to run down my cheeks. One of the other men from across the hall heard all the commotion and came running over. He said. "What's going on? What's the matter with your friend?"

I didn't answer.

He nonchalantly looked at Mac and said, "O my God, I think your friend is dead. We better get some help."

The man immediate ran up to the corner where a policeman was directing traffic and told him about Mac. I couldn't move. I just kneeled there, looking at my friend in disbelief. How much can one man endure. The policeman called for an ambulance that took him to the morgue.

11

A Search for Family

Once the ambulance left, I began to run as fast as my legs would carry me to the Shelter. When I arrived, I saw Larry, whowas still in the dining hall having a cup of coffee. I came rushing towards him like a man on fire.

Larry grabbed my arm and said "Professor what's going on. Where are you going in such a rush?"

"He did it, Larry. He finally got his wish. Mac's dead."

Larry quickly got up from his seat and hugged me. Tears began to stream down his face. Larry loved Mac as much as I did. Even more. We were the only family Larry never knew. The family he wished for. "O shit. That's terrible Professor. I don't know what to say."

I suddenly became angry. "Dam it all. I know. We were so close to getting him help. He had agreed to see the doctor today. So close."

I brushed his arm away from me and said "Can't talk now. I Can't. I have to see Mary about Mac. I'll talk to you later."

I hurried to Mary's office and found that her door was closed. She was meeting with a client. Having no regard for her privacy, I burst through the door and started yelling. "Mary. Mary. Have you heard the news? Mac is dead."

Mary became angry. She turned towards me and said. "Mr. Byrne what is the meaning of this.? Can't you see that I have a client?"

She hadn't been told about the news of Mac's death. I said. "The hell with the client. Mac is dead. He's dead Mary."

She quickly saw how upset I was thus excused herself, ushered out her client and closed the door.

With a puzzled look on her face she said. "What do you mean he's dead?"

I was still out or breath from running. "When I went back to the factory to take Mac to the clinic this morning, I found him dead." I started to yell. "I couldn't save him. I can't save anyone. Everybody around me ends up dead." I began to cry uncontrollable. Mary put her arms around me and gently moved me onto a chair near her desk. "Gregory, sit down. Let me get you a glass of water."

She went to her desk and poured a glass of water from a pitcher.

"Here, take this?"

I hurriedly drank the water and said, "You have to do something?"

She was puzzled by my request. "What do you mean do something? Isn't he dead? What can I do?"

I rapidly began talking about what has to be done. My words were coming out of my mouth so fast, that Mary had trouble understanding what I was saying.

"He has two daughters, you need to call them. I know they'd want to see their father. I know Mac would want them here. We have to make funeral arrangements. What about a funeral home?"

"Gregory slow down, I can hardly understand what your trying to say. Certainly, we can make funeral arrangements if need be. But you said he has two daughters? Do you know where they are or where they live?"

I was becoming more upset and in a panic. "Shit Mary, I don't know where they live. I took a picture of them from Mac's coat before they took him away. I mean, can't you get someone to find them. It's important."

"Calm down Greg. Take it easy. I have a few friends in the Boston Police Dept. There's one person I know very well. He's helped me with problems like this in the past, a detective. Maybe I can ask him to find family."

"Maybe this picture will help find them. Wait a minute, at times he did mention something about a Waltham or Woburn. Some place like that."

"Don't worry Gregory. We're going to find his daughters. I'll call my friend Mike O'Rourke right now and let him know what we have. I can give him the picture and let him know what you said."

"Great. Great Mary. That's wonderful."

"Okay sit down and let me call him now"

Mary called her friend Mike and gave him all the details. He said he would do his best to locate them, his daughters. He thought it wouldn't be a problem.

She then turned to me and said. "All we can do now Greg is wait. I'll let you know something as soon as I hear from Mike. It might take a few days. Be patient Greg. Right know I'm worried about you."

"I can't do this therapy or counseling stuff anymore. I just can't."

"Okay. Okay. Maybe we can talk about that later. For now, why you don't stay at the shelter."

I was confused by her offer. "But were supposed to leave this place during the day, aren't we?"

"Don't worry. There's an empty room down at the end of the hall with a cot in it. Why don't you go down there and try and rest?"

"I don't know If I can."

"Just try. I'll have the doctor, who should be in at 9:00 to give you something to settle your nervous."

I gave a deep sigh and said, "Thanks Mary. I'm sorry for being so angry or nasty, I'm sorry for acting like a crazy man."

"I know you're very upset. Mac meant a lot to you."

12

THE FUNERAL

It took three weeks before the police were able to track down Mac's daughters. Finding their father was a mixed blessing for them. They were both saddened over his death but elated about finding him. They quickly made funeral preparations for their father and had a mass at the Cathedral in Boston. His daughters had been frantically searching for him since the day he eloped from the hospital. After years of searching, they assumed that he might have committed suicide but never gave up on the search. They loved their dad and were worried sick about him when he went missing. When they first received a visit from the detective they felt hopeful that their father was still alive. That little spark of hope was soon extinguished when they saw the look on detective O'Rourke's face. His older daughters Katherine Rawlins was married and living in Newton. She had three young boys. His second daughter Margaret McIntyre was single and living in New York. She was a Vice-President of a marketing company. These two beautiful daughters, became very upset when they received the news.

There was no wake but a reception line was held at the back of the church which was later followed by a luncheon at a local restaurant. Mary, my social worker along with myself and Larry attended the service and luncheon. I didn't feel it was right for me to show up in my smelly tattered clothes but Mary was able to find some suitable clothing for myself and Larry. The reception line was graced by his daughters and their family, including the grandchildren. I couldn't help thinking to myself. *if only Mac could see his beautiful family.* I couldn't understand why he left his lovely family for a life of being homeless. But then I thought to myself. *Didn't you do the same thing?*

The first of his family I talked to, was his single daughter Margaret. She was a strikingly beautiful woman with a trim figure, long blonde hair and blue eyes. I approached her with a hug and said. "I knew you dad very well. We shared the same place. I can tell you one thing without reservation, he loved you and your sister dearly."

I than took Mac's picture of the family out of my vest-pocket and presented it to her. I continued to say that. "He always kept that picture with him. I tried to get him help with his medical condition but he always resisted my attempts until the day I found him dead. I'm so sorry. I wish I had tried harder."

A smile adorned her face. "No need to be sorry. I know my father. He was always a very stubborn man. I thank you for your kindness and being a good friend to him." The sadness I felt at that very moment permeated my whole body.

Her eyes were reddened from crying but she continued to talk about her dad. "You probably know that dad was upset not only about the job but my mom's passing. I can't begin to tell you how much he loved her. He was never the same after her death. What happened at the job was the last straw. I knew that he didn't want to live anymore. Life was too much for him. In many ways this was not such a big surprise."

"Yes, he did relate to me how upset he was about your mom's death and the job. No matter what I said, I couldn't do anything to take away the guilt that he felt about what happened on the job. He always blamed himself, for the death of those people."

She than introduced me along with Mary and Larry to the rest of her family. As I was leaving the reception line, she tapped me on the shoulder and said. "Maybe we can talk a little more about dad at the luncheon. I'd like to know more about him."

"I'd be more than happy to."

We went to the grave site and said our final goodbyes. His daughters had decided to have him cremated and placed his ashes in the ground with a plaque which had his name, the date of his birth and death along with his wife's name. A simple few words were at the bottom of the plaque which said, *we love you daddy.* The ground also held a second plaque, which was that of his wife.

Margaret turned to me and said. "They're finally back together again. I know they're happy now."

Following the trip to the cemetery, we proceeded to go to the restaurant where they had an open bar and a wonderful meal. It had been a very long time since I had such a meal, a real meal. I restrained myself from having any alcohol. I wanted to honor Mac's memory. Instead of a drink, I had a ginger ale.

I began talking to the rest of family by saying. "Your father was a kind and gentle man. He was always concerned about all of us. I was having these horrible nightmares and he along with Larry got me the help I needed. He was a hard guy to say no to."

Than Katherine said, "So Greg, you still have a family?"

I wasn't quite sure how to answer her because of Mac deserting his own family. I stumble around for the words and finally replied. "Yes. I have a daughter and I'm separated from my wife and I have only one brother and my mother."

A look of anger came over her face. "And do they know where you are?"

I was taken aback by her question especially after the hurt they had experienced when Mac left his family. I didn't know how to answer her. My head dropped to my chest in shame as I sheepishly said. "No"

Her anger now began to escalate as she scolded me for leaving my family.

"How could you do that to your family? Can't you see what my father did to us and then died. Your family is probably worried sick. Wondering what the hell happened to you. Why would you want to torment your family like that?"

"I wasn't a good father or husband. I did a bad thing. I was no good to them."

"No matter what happened in the past, I'm sure your family wants you back in their life. You can't desert them. Do you know how much pain you're causing them? What the hell's the matter with you?"

Her husband witnessing his wife' upset, put his arm around her and said. "Kathy? Come on. Settle down. Greg isn't our business. Sorry Greg."

I got up from the table and quickly left. Mary came running after me before I got to the exit. "Gregory. Try to understand. She was very upset about her father and the funeral. Please don't take it to heart. Why don't we go back to the office and talk about it?"

"Thanks Mary but I can't do that now. Maybe tomorrow. You know she's right. I should return home but I just can't. I'm not ready."

"I understand. That's why it's important for us to continue our sessions."

I didn't say a word but just kept running away from the restaurant until I was back at the factory. I knew that the only way home would be through Mary my social worker. Mary was my only hope.

13

AFTER THE FUNERAL

Larry returned from the restaurant shortly after I left. He was very concerned about me. When he entered our space, he said. "Professor. You Okay? What happened in there? I couldn't believe that Kathrine, Mac's daughter, would jump all over you like that."

"She completely caught me off guard Larry. But she had a point. How could I argue with her? What she said is the truth."

"So, what are you going to do"

"I'll be seeing Mary tomorrow. No matter what happens in our sessions, I'm going to stay with my therapy. No more walking out on her. It's time I face my problems and deal with them."

I just wanted to go to sleep but Larry kept throwing questions at me.

"Do you ever think you'll go back to your family?"

"That's my goal. Okay Larry. Enough is enough. Let me get some sleep. I'm emotionally spent. It's been a long day. We can talk tomorrow when we go to the shelter for breakfast."

"Of course. Sorry for all the questions."

We both turned into our beds composed of cardboard and old blankets. I didn't go to the shelter that night but decided to stay at the factory. But my sleep was again interrupted by my old nightmares. It wasn't a pleasant sleep by all means.

I wondered what tomorrow would bring. Would I ever see my family again or will I end up dead, like mac?

The next morning, Larry and I went to the shelter for a hot breakfast. Once we were seated, Larry began asking questions, where he left off. You seeing Mary this morning?"

"Yes, right after breakfast."

He then turned to me and said. "Seems strange waking up in the morning and not seeing Mac. Now it's just the two of us."

"I know it. I miss him, already. I feel so bad and guilty. I should have been more forceful with Mac about getting help."

Larry put his arm on my shoulder in an attempt comfort me. "Hey Professor. It is, what it is. The man wanted to die. He was finished with life. You weren't going to stop him."

I shook my head. "Maybe you're right Larry, maybe you're right."

I gave out a little laugh at Larry's remarks. "Larry, you have a lot of smarts for a young man."

Larry laughed. "You call it wisdom. I call it experience. I had more than my share of a shitty life."

"You're a smart kid. You still have time to turn around your life. You're no dummy. And you're a nice guy."

He laughed again. "Thanks Professor. I appreciate that. Maybe someday I'll do just that. If I had a father, he would be just like you. You are the dad I never had."

"Thanks Larry."

"And another thing Professor, you better stick around. At least until you go home."

"Don't worry about that I'm not going anywhere in a hurry." I gave him a hug and said. "I'll always be there for you, wherever I am"."

"So, Professor, are you going for your appointment with Mary? It's getting late?"

"Thanks for the reminder. My appointment is in a few minutes. Don't want to be late. You know Larry, you should give her a try. I think you'll like her.

"I just might give it a try someday."

"Never mind someday. Do it now."

"I'll think about it. Right now, I have to hit the streets. I'm running low on cash. See you at the factory this afternoon."

"Okay Larry, stay safe."

"Will do Professor."

14

THE NEED TO TALK

I turned in my breakfast tray and walked over to Mary's office. I knocked on the door and was warmly greeted by her. "Greg, I'm so glad to see you. I know it's been rough with the loss of your friend Mac. And yesterday, at the funeral, just added to your problems."

"I can't help thinking about Mac. We were all so close. I tried to save him but I couldn't. Seems like everyone important in my life dies, between Mac and my father."

"Greg, you shouldn't blame yourself for Mac's death. He wanted to die. You tried your best. But you're alive and have for a good life."

"I don't know Mary. Maybe you're right."

"In order for you to begin your journey to a better life, you need to talk to me. Why don't be begin by talking about your dad's death. Talk is where the healing can start. Why don't you continue where you left off with your father?"

"I'll try."

"Relax and close your eyes. Take a deep breath. What happened Gregory ? Tell me about it."

"I was about 12 years old at the time and my brother was 19. After high school my brother Frank went to work for dad. My father tried to persuade him to go to college, but that's not what Frank wanted to do. He loved the business and carpentry as much as my dad.

They were working on a house in Framingham on a warm and sunny day in May when it happened. It was about 6:50 pm when they were getting ready to pack up their gear and go home. Suddenly, a loose timber from above came crashing" .... There was a pause.... "And it... killed him."

"I am so sorry Gregory. That was terrible, to lose your dad at such a young age?"

"The worse part, it was a stupid accident. The two by four hit his head at such an angle, that it instantly killed him. My father has had many close calls from falling off a roof to getting hit with a hammer but he always managed to survive those accidents."

"So how did you feel after it happened?"

"Terrible doesn't begin to describe how I felt and am still feeling. I never got over it. The memory of that accident continues to haunt me"

"How did you find out about the accident?"

"It was a Thursday afternoon when the school Secretary called me out of my math class. I was puzzled. I knew I didn't do anything wrong. At least I hoped I didn't. But why was she calling me out of class? When I got to the office, she handed me the phone. It was my brother. He said there was a bad accident at the worksite. His voice was shaking and he had trouble getting the words out of his mouth. I became very nervous and I cautiously asked him, if everyone was okay? I guess I was looking for some assurance that the news wasn't really bad. The phone went silent on the other end of the line. He then said. "No, things are not okay. There was an accident. They rushed him to the hospital."

I started yelling at him. "Frank, is dad okay. Can I go see him at the hospital?"

He didn't want to tell me of my father's death over the phone. He said he would come to school and pick me up. When we got home, he told me that our father was dead. I felt like someone had punched me in the stomach. I became nauseous and threw up.

I began to cry uncontrollable and yelling at God. My dad was such a good Catholic always made sure that we went to church. I didn't understand how God would do this to me. I said, "God why did you take him? He was a good man. Always made sure we went to church. Why? Why? My brother tried to comfort me but was not successful."

Tears began to stream down the side of my face as I recalled that awful day, the day I lost my dad.

Mary than handed me a tissue to dry the tears from my face."

I than related in anger. "First the bitch of a mother leaves us and then the person I cared of the most dies. At that point in time, I thought that my life was over, gone. But my brother was like a rock. He pulled me through it. He became my dad and brought me up, all on his own."

"So, your brother was always an important person in your life, especially at the accident? He was always there for you, through all those terrible tragedies."

"You'll never know how much he means to me. Never."

"Does your brother know where you are?"

"No. And I don't want him to know. I don't want him to see me like this."

I became very upset. I thought I had all that shit under control but I didn't. The pain was still with me. I got up from my chair and began walking to the office door. "I have to leave. I have to."

Mary said. I know you're hurting but you have to stop running away from your pain and troubles."

"I guess you're right. You, know this was the first time I shared my feelings with anyone about dad's death."

"And how does it feel to share those feelings?"

"I paused for a few moments and said. "Not too bad. In some ways I feel a sense of relief."

"Good. You've just taken your first step towards healing. Congratulations."

15

HELP FROM A STRANGER

The next day, it was early in the afternoon. The rain was hitting the factory roof like a man playing a metal drum. Larry and I decided to spend the day inside to avoid the bad weather. We were hoping that the inclement weather would subside so thst we could go for dinner at the shelter. We sat down on the office desk, pulled up a couple of broken chairs and began playing rummy. We had closed the door to our space, since we didn't want any interruptions. It was peacefully quiet since most of the other homeless were out panhandling in the rain.

It was about 4:00pm when I said to Larry. "Sounds like the rain has let up."

"Yes, I think you're right." The lack of rain on the factory's tin roof came to an eerie silence. It was like the whole world was absent but only for a brief moment."

"Okay Larry let's make a run for it."

As we began to exit our space, we were confronted by three young men, maybe in the earlier twenties. You could tell by their clothing, that they were not homeless. One guy was wearing Air-Jordan sneakers. Another guy had a gold chain around his neck and the third young man wore an expensive pair of jeans. I could see that they were trouble. A group of young people looking to hassle some homeless guys. This was their idea of having fun. We tried to move pass then, when the guy with the golden chain named The Boss said. "Hey guys where're are you going? Don't you want to party with us? Have a little fun?"

I said, "We just want to go to the shelter for some dinner. We're not looking for any trouble".

The guy with the expensive jeans said, "Did you hear that boss, they want to go have their din, din?"

His comments caused an eruption of laughter from the group.

"You know what Jackson, maybe we can give them some dinner right here." He pointed to a brown pile of feces, which was behind him. "Look what I found Jackson shit pie. It looks so good." He pointed to Larry and said "You should have yourself a taste. Get down on your knees and lap some of it up. Real good and tasty."

I reacted by saying. "Leave him alone. Just let us go."

"Look Jackson, a hero. A piece of garbage, coming to the defense of the poor girly kid. He's so fragile that he can't defend himself. What a pussy."

He then turned to the third member of the group, the one with the gold chain and said "Goldie, help the little pussy have himself a real treat."

Larry tried to resist but Goldie pushed his face into the shit while Larry was screaming and trying to resist.

They all began to laugh as Larry struggled to break loose.

I'm not a very aggressive guy. Never was. As a matter of fact, I was always very passive. Never had to defend myself. My brother was the fighter, my defender. But I couldn't take their bullying any longer. So, I sprang to my feet and threw my body at Goldie, which sent him flying to the bug infested ground. When he got up, he was red-faced mad. He came charging at me like a raging bull. When, he came towards me, I moved to the side, and pushed him to the ground again where upon he hit his head on a stray concrete block. The block caused blood to come gushing out of the side of his head. It was then time, for the rest of the gang to come at me and Larry. They began throwing punches at us that we couldn't defend against. One hit me in the nose which caused it to bleed and another punch to my stomach put me on the ground. Both Larry and I were bleeding badly and laying on the ground. They then proceeded to kick us. They were in a state of rage. It was at that very moment that another man in his thirties about five feet ten and an athletic built came on the scene. He was armed with a two by four which he used on both the Boss and Goldie before they could defend themselves. The other gang member, Jackson than rushed him in an attempt to defend his friends but he was no match for this guy, who kept hitting him in the face and stomach. When Jackson fell to the ground, he began kicking and kicking him.

The three of them scrambled to their feet as quick as they could and ran out of the building. The stranger than helped both Larry and myself up on our feet and said. "You guys okay? You look like you're in tough shape. You're bleeding all over the place."

He then took a hankie from his jacket and gave it to us to wipe the blood off our faces.

I responded to him while grimacing from the pain that was inflicted on me. "Hurting but we'll be okay. We have to thank you man. If it were not for you, they probably would have killed us." I replied breathless.

He then said. No problem. I hate scumbags like them. Why don't you go to the shelter? They always have a nurse on duty that could help you."

I said, "So you go to the shelter? We were just on our way when these guys came after us."

"No, I don't do shelters but maybe I could hang with you here at the factory, if that's all right. Been looking for a place.?"

I quickly replied. "Are you kidding? Sure, you can. You saved our butts. By the way, what's your name?"

"I'm Nick and you?"

"I'm called the Professor but my real name is Gregory. And this is my friend Larry."

"Well, why don't you two, get yourself fixed up."

"Sure, we can't convince you to come with us? The food is pretty good at the shelter."

"Thanks for the invite but no thanks. But if you want, you can bring me something to eat."

"Not a problem. Be happy to get some food for you."

"What's your name?"

"Nick."

"Okay Nick. Larry, let's get moving."

"Sure."

"As we left the factory, torrential rains were drenching us through our clothing but it felt good to be alive.

Larry turned to me and said. "Man, he's one tough guy. See the way he handled those goons?"

"Looks like he knows how to take care of himself. I'm sure he's been in many a scrape during his lifetime."

"Well Professor, that's what worries me. You sure you want him to stay with us?"

"Come on Larry. The guy saved our asses. I think he'll be okay. Be nice to have some company." Larry wasn't fully convinced.

That evening we all slept quietly in the factory without incident. Nick proved to be an interesting person but like all of us, he had his own problems.

16

MY FATHER'S FUNERAL

The next day I went to see Mary. When I sat down in her office, she couldn't help but notice the bruises on my face.

She was shocked when she saw how messed up my face was since she knew I wasn't the kind of guy that would get into a fight. Mary was very concerned about me. I could see it on her face. "Greg what happened to you? Your face looks like you were in a fight."

"Well, you have that right. Me and Larry were accosted by these three goons. If this guy named Nick didn't come along, I wouldn't be meeting with you today."

"So, what happened?"

I then related to her what happened to us.

"I'm sorry to hear that Greg. You okay? You feel like talking?"

"I'm fine. I went to the clinic and the doc took care of me and Larry."

"And what about Nick? Did he go with you?"

"No. He said, he doesn't like shelters but he's staying with us at the factory."

"Okay. Well I'm' happy you're all right. Let's see. The last time we met, we talked about your father. You were pretty upset when we started to talk about his death. Why don't you begin by telling me a little about the funeral? Were they many people? Relatives. friends."

"Not many people. The guys from my father's company came to pay their respect and of course my grandparents flew in from Texas and a few aunts and uncles from Maryland. And of course, Mr. Perkins from my school came."

"Mr. Perkins? Sounds like Mr. Perkins was a special person in your life."

"He was, a very special person. I couldn't have survived High School without his help. He was one of the reasons I went into teaching."

I than turned the conversation back to the funeral. "So, you can see, we're a small family. My dad was an only child and my grandfather had just one brother. Now on my mother's side, she had two sisters. They all made it to the funeral. My grandparents had to travel from Texas and my aunts and uncle came from Maryland and New Jersey. Our family is scattered all over the place."

"Did any of your family stay to help out?"

"No. But I can't fault them. You know, we were never very close to my relatives. Dad had left home after graduating from High School and went East. My grandparents were never happy about his moving away. They wanted him to stay in Texas and learn the business. But that was not dad's cup of tea. He wanted to explore the East coast."

"Did they ever visit you?"

"Not very much. Sure, we would see them maybe once or twice a year during a holiday but that was it."

"So, what was it like when all your company had gone and it was just you and your brother?"

"Not so good. My brother Frank was immobilized for two days. He just couldn't move. And me, I cried myself to sleep for a week."

"What about your father's business?"

"Fortunately, Hank Rawlins, the supervisor for my father took right over for Frank. When Frank finally realized that dad was dead and he was now in charge, he began to come to life. A big construction business was an immense responsibility to place on a young twenty-year-old man. Sure, he worked for dad but he didn't know much about how to run the business. That's where Hank Rawlins was a big help. He showed him what to do. How to keep the books. Introduced him to the accountant. Where to order building materials. Told him about my father's jobs that were outstanding, and so on. It was a lot to take in but Frank was a fast learner."

"And what about you?"

I than related to Mary how I dealt with my fathers' death. "I hadn't been to school for three days. I just couldn't move myself to do anything. This one day, I was watching television in the living room, in my pajamas. Didn't have any desire to get dressed or cleaned. Frank called me into the kitchen and sat me down. He had a very serious, no nonsense-look on his face when he said. "Greg, we need to talk."

"I turned my head away from him and said. "I don't want to talk. I just want to go back to watching television."

Frank began to get angry with me. "No. You're not going anywhere. We're going to talk."

"About what. There's nothing to say. My life is over. Dad's dead. End of story."

"No, your life's not over. You, me, we need to get on with the business of living. Tomorrow you're going back to school. You've already missed more time than you should have."

I became defiant. "You crazy Frank? I'm not going back to school. I can work for you."

"That's not an option. I said you're going back to school. That's it. End of discussion."

I than returned his angry. I got up from my chair and started yelling at him. "What's the matter with you Frank? You don't feel nothing about dad? Don't you miss him? You act as if nothing happened. Same old business."

My comments sent my brother into a rage. He got up from his seat and began shaking me. "You little bastard. You think you're the only one whose hurting? Don't you think I feel his loss? That it's hard for me to go on without him?" For the first time in my life, I saw Frank cry. Tears came streaming down his cheeks. "Shit, I miss him. I miss him more than you'll ever know. I'm stuck with a business which I don't know how to run. This business that we need to put food on the table and a roof over our heads. I don't have the luxury of staying in bed or spend my days watching television and feeling sorry for myself. Don't you think if dad was standing right there beside us that he would tell us to get off our ass and start living again. There are things to be done. Do you hear me?

You're going back to school and do chores around

the house. You hear me? We can hire a new housekeeper to help with the cleaning and cooking, but you need to do some chores like cutting the lawn and trimming the bushes. And keeping your own space clean. Do you understand what I'm saying?"

I had never seen Frank so angry and emotional in all my life. I couldn't answer him. All I could do was cry. When Frank saw the tears cascading down my face, he took me in his arms and held me close to his muscular chest and said in a soft comforting voice... "I know it's hard Greg. I know. But its' time we return to the business of living."

The next morning, I got up early and went to school.

17

WHAT'S NEXT?

M ary turned to me and said, "So what happened next? What was it like when you went back to school?"

I was 15 years old and a Sophomore. I really had no friends. Not only did I not have friends but sometimes I was the target of bullying by some of the football players. But all people, even the football players, knew what had happened and expressed their condolences. The one person who truly offered me comfort was my Social Studies Teacher Mr. Roger Perkins.

That first day in class he approached me.

"Gregory, I'm so happy to see you back in school."

I didn't say much except to grunt and say "Yes."

"I have a free period after this class would you like to talk to me?"

With my face looking down at the floor I replied. "I don't know."

"If you want, I'll be in my office. I just bought some knew books on pre-industrial societies. I know you had an interest in the topic. One in particular has to do with human sacrifices. You can borrow them if you like. I won't be able to get at them for some time. Or we can just talk about things. Whatever you want."

"I'll see."

I desperately needed to talk to someone beside Frank so I decided to take him up on his invitation. I often times wondered if he bought those books for himself or for me. He was that kind of a guy. Always ready to help his students.

When I arrived at his office, he warmly greeted me. "I'm glad you decided to come. Before, I forget, takes these books and keep them for as long as you'd like."

"You sure."

"Positive. I have so much work to do. It'll be months before I get to them."

"Thanks, Mr. Perkins."

"Again, I want to say "How sorry I am about the death of your father. I know he meant the world to you." everything to you.

"Yes."

"Now your brother has taken over the construction business?"

"Yes."

"Not very talkative today. Usually you chew my ears off and pepper me with a hundred questions."

"Mr. Perkins, I don't want to be rude but could we talk about something else?"

"I'm sorry. Of course, we can. What would you like to talk about?"

"I was thinking that I'd like to become a teacher. Like you."

"Really. You won't make much money."

"I don't care about the money. My brother said. It

was my choice. That after High School, I could go on to college but he didn't want me to work in the construction business with him. Do you think I'd make a good teacher?"

"Of course, I do. You'd make an excellent teacher. I'm surprised of your interest in teaching. I know you love the subject but a teacher."

"Is it hard? Do you think I could do it.?"

"Absolutely. You're a good student. You work hard and have been on the on the honor role. I'd be more than happy to write a recommendation for you."

"Thanks. Where should I go to school? I mean money might be an issue."

"You have several good choices with state schools which are affordable. Places like Bridgewater and Fitchburg State."

"Thanks Mr. Perkins. I really appreciate your help."

"Anytime. Anytime you want to talk, you're always welcome."

I left his office feeling renewed like I just got another shot at life. The idea of college suddenly seemed attractive to me. Mr. Perkins always made me feel good. I left his office feeling hopeful. I thought to myself that it was time to get back to the business of living, just like my brother Frank had told me.

As I was walking home, I couldn't help but look towards the sky where I saw a bird. It was an omen for the future. I looked at the bird as it traversed the background of the blue sky and said. "I'm going to make it dad. I'm going to make you proud."

I ran home to tell Frank about my new-found hope and my decision to go to college.

18

The Good News

When I finally reached home, I couldn't wait to tell Frank about my decision to go to college and become a teacher. It was only 4:30 and I knew I wouldn't see Frank until 6:30pm, if I was lucky. If he had to work late and then I wouldn't able to see him until, 7:00pm or even later.

Frank worked long hours so I decided to surprise him by making supper. I never really cooked before and didn't know where to begin. Then I got an idea. I could make him macaroni. How hard could it be? I looked through the cabinet until I spied a box of penne pasta and a jar of tomato sauce. I had seen him make garlic bread by putting oil on bread and baking it in the oven. *This will be a piece of cake* I thought to myself. So, I thought. I waited until about 6:30 before I began my unholy cooking project. I carefully read the directions which told me to boil the water and when bubbles appeared, place the pasta in it. The sauce was even easier. I just had to place the sauce in a pot and turn on the stove's top burner. With the bread, I covered it with oil and liberally sprinkled some garlic powder on it. While the water was boiling, I placed the bread on a tray and put it in the oven. I was feeling so proud of myself. I had actually made dinner all by myself, without my brother's help. Everything was going like planned. I carefully set the table with some dishes and utensils and poured some water in my glass and would later get a beer for my brother.

I then went into the living room and began watching television. I guess all the excitement of the day caused me to fall asleep while my supper was cooking. After about 25 minutes, I heard Frank, come running into the kitchen screaming. "What the hell is going on Greg. What's all the smoke."

Frank's yelling, abruptly woke me from my reverie. Still half asleep, I said, "What?" I then smelled the burnt bread and smoke coming from the kitchen.

When Frank opened the oven, the smoke came pouring out. The sauce had creeped over the side of the pot and covered the top of the stove. The water from the pot had spilled on to the stove, mixing with the red sauce and the pasta laid on the stove lifeless and limp.

I than became upset and tried to explain to my brother my good intentions. "I tried to make dinner and fell asleep. I'm sorry Frank"

Frank grabbed a dishtowel and began to fan the smoke out of the open window. "Shit Greg. You could have burnt the place down."

My brother's' anger caused me to cry as I tried to speak. "I was just trying to surprise you for supper."

Frank suddenly burst into a laughter. "Okay kid. Come here. I really appreciate what you tried to do. Sorry for getting so angry at you. It just scared me. That's all we needed was a house fire. Sorry."

"What are we going to do for dinner now that I screwed up our supper?"

"I have an idea. Why don't I have some pizza delivered for supper? Sound good?"

I went over and hugged him. "Thanks Frank. You're the best."

Frank went to this phone and ordered pizza and a salad.

As we sat down at the table and ate once the pizza was ordered Frank turned to me and said. "So, tell me what was the occasion for supper Greg?"

You remember how you told me that it was time to start living?

Well, I went to talk to Mr., Perkins."

"Who's he?"

"My social studies teacher. I told him I wanted to become a teacher. He thought it was a great idea."

Frank quickly developed a very surprised look on his face. "A teacher? Really?" He jokingly said. "So, you don't want to work in the business with me?"

I laughed and said. "No construction for me. I really want to teach. I love social studies and think I could do a good job."

As always, Frank was very encouraging. "So that means that next year, we'll have to go looking at some colleges. Right?"

A smile graced my face and I said "That's what it looks like."

And laughing he said. "I also think, we need to hire someone to do our cooking and cleaning. Neither one of us will survive without help. Look at this place, the dust is piling up and there's crap all over the house. You'd think two bachelors lived here."

"But can we afford it Frank?"

"We have no choice. You might try cooking again and burn down the house."

We both broke into laughter

"Tomorrow I'll start asking round for someone."

19

THE SEARCH

A few days later, Frank came home earlier from works since he had decided to interview a few people for the job of housekeeper. He asked me to stay skip school since he wanted me to be a part of the process. Frank always included me in making family decisions. He said we were a team and since we will be spending a lot of time with this woman or man, I should have a say in who we choose. It made me feel like an adult and not some High School Sophomore.

The first person we interviewed was a single woman in her fifties, who came with a rigid set of does and don'ts. I immediately didn't like her not did Frank. I felt that she was interviewing us rather than us interviewing her.

Her name was Rachael Honeyberry. She said she had plenty of experience as a housekeeper, cook and nannie. Well, I didn't think we needed someone who was going to treat me like a young child. She provided us with some very impressive references from people who utilized her more as a nannie than a housekeeper.

We wanted someone to run the household not someone who would be running our lives.

The next woman who came into the house, was a woman in her forties, who was married and had three children. She immediately told us that there would be times when she'd have to tend to her own family. We thanked her for her time but never called her back.

We went through four other people, who had great credentials, but we believed that their personalities would not be compatible with us and our life styles.

Frank turned to me after the last person left and said. "This should have been a lot easier. I didn't expect it to be so hard."

"I know. Do we have anyone else coming?"

At this point in the day, we were feeling very discouraged.

The last person to apply for the job was a woman by the name of Mrs. O'Shea, who lived in East Arlington. She was markedly different than any of the other people. To beginning with, she was in her early sixties, had no references and had never done this kind of work. We were very puzzled as to why she would even apply for such a job.

Frank began the interview. "Mrs. O'Shea. I guess I'm a little puzzled as to why you applied for the position. I would have thought you might be retiring rather than starting a new job."

She took offense to Frank's comments. "Let me tell you something young man, I might be in my sixties but I'm not ready for a nursing home or the graveyard."

Frank was taken aback by her response. He began to stutter. "I'm.. sorr... Mrs. O'Shea. I didn't mean to offend you."

"Apology accepted. Now to the business as to why I applied. I lost my husband a year ago from a freak car accident. He was my life since we couldn't have any children. I always wanted children but the good Lord said no, not for me. After hanging around the house for a year, I prayed to the Lord to send me something to make my life more fulfilling. This seemed to be the perfect answer to my prayers."

Frank continued in his questioning. "You seem like a very religious person."

"That I am and I assume you are God fearing people?"

Frank didn't know how to respond to Mrs. O'Shea since the both of us had stopped going to church after my dad died. I guess we were both angry with God, who took our dad.

Frank tried to gloss over the question. "Yes, we are God fearing. Now there's a lot of work to get done. We're not the cleanest guys in the world. We've been bachelors for some time ever since our dad had died and....."

Before Frank could finish his sentence, Mrs. O'Shea broke into laughter.

"Don't be fooled by my age. Like I said, I'm not ready to be placed in a nursing home. I can handle any kind of job from scrubbing floors to washing down the bathroom to cooking up a storm."

"Really?"

"Let me tell you two youngsters, I can out work the both of you."

Her remarks sent us into roaring laughter.

Frank continued. "And what do you like to cook."

"Anything you want. I'm Irish, born in Ireland and

came to this country when I was a wee little girl but I learned how to cook all kinds of food especially Italian. My husband was Italian, God bless his soul. How's that for a menu?"

The both of us fell in love with this lady's spirit and spunk.

"And you don't have any reference?"

"I have none. My only reference is caring for my husband for 40 years. That is my reference, except for what I'm telling you. I never worked a day in my life, my husband was the breadwinner so I had no need of a job"

"No references. Never worked."

"That's right but I'll give you 100%. You can bet on that. If you don't like my work, feel free to let me go."

Frank looked at me with a grin on his face as if to say what do you think. I nodded and Frank said. "You know what, you have the job.

From that day on, Mrs. O'Shea became an important part of our life.

20

MRS. O'SHEA

The first day I came home from school after hiring Mrs. O'Shea, I saw a plate of brownies on the table with a tall glass of cold milk. Mrs. O'Shea was busily preparing dinner, as she stood by the stove. The smell of the lamb stew teased my nostrils. We had never eaten lamb in all our lives. Certainly not with my mother.

When I saw the brownies on the table I said, "What's with the brownies and the milk? Who are they for?"

She gave me a puzzled look and said. "For you. Who Else would I be baking it for? Sit down and eat and then you can go right upstairs and do your homework."

"The brownies are for me? Do my homework?" No one had ever told me to do my homework and my mother certainly was not the homemaker type. I was shocked. After stumbling over my words, I said. "Sure, I'll do my homework. But these are for me?"

"O. Lord boy, who else would they be for?"

"Thank you. Thank you. My mother never did any baking for me. She divorced my dad and left him for another man. She was a real bitch."

Mrs. O'Shea suddenly became very angry. Her face turned red like the color of a firetruck. "What did you say? I should be taking you over my knee and giving you a spanking, no matter how old you are. I never want to hear such language in this house again. Do you hear me boy?"

I began to stutter. "Yes... Mam....I'm...sorry. I didn't mean to talk like that."

"That's better. If you want to get some more of my baking, I better not hear such language ever again. And you better do well in school and behave yourself."

"Yes Mam."

Mrs. O'Shea came to this country many years ago but her voices still had a sweet Irish lilt to it, when she spoke. I loved it.

"Listen boy, no matter what she was, she is your mother and you need to respect her for it. She was the one who brought you into this world. Remember that."

"Yes mam." I took some of the brownies and a glass of milk and went directly up to my room as ordered, to do my homework.

It was about 6:30pm, when Frank came through the door and he was immediately taken by the delicious smell of the lamb stew. It had been a long time since we enjoyed real home cooking.

Frank had not taken off his coat and work boots as he walked into the kitchen. "Wow. What is that beautiful smell and aroma. It smells like something from my distant past. I think they called It real home cooking."

I was in the living room watching TV and yelled, "Its lamb stew Frank. Can you believe it?"

"It's like nothing I ever smelled before."

Mrs. O'Shea than turned to Frank with her hands

on her hips just as he was about to walk into the living room.

She immediately confronted him and said. "If you want to enjoy more of my cooking, you need to leave your boots at the door. You'll not be tracking mud and debris on my clean floors with those dirty boots. From now on, leave your boots and shoes at the door. And that goes for you to boy."

Frank didn't know what to do or say. Anyways, how could he argue with her. She was right. We soon began to understand the rules of Mrs. O'Shea. Once we washed up for dinner and sat down to eat, I lifted up the ladle to fill my dish, when a small wrinkled hand smacked my wrist. It was Mrs. O'Shea. She chastised me for not saying grace before we eat. "Now Frank and Gregory, we first need to give thanks to the Lord for this wonderful meal. We will be giving thanks before every meal. Do you boys understand me?"

We both responded by saying "Yes mam."

Frank restrained himself from laughing. She said grace and we all ate.

Our lives were changed dramatically with the entrance of Mrs. O'Shea. We soon came to learn of Mrs. O'Shea and her rules.

21

TIME PASSES

Time has a way of passing with or without you. My Junior year soon presented itself and it was time to look at colleges. Frank again took a day off from work and made appointments to take me to visit a few schools. It was a Saturday morning after Mrs. O'Shea had made us a hearty breakfast of eggs, bagels, home fries and bacon. Following the meal, she instructed us to clear the table, which became a part of our routine. It was another one of Mrs. O'Shea's rules.

We both thanked her for breakfast and then Frank turned to me and said. "You ready Greg? Why don't we start with Boston College."

As Mrs. O'Shea was doing the dishes she said. "Now that's a good Catholic school." She had an opinion about everything.

Frank quickly responded. Yes, it is and a good school academically with an excellent reputation. What do you say Greg?"

"But Frank, that's a private school."

Frank just shook his head and said. "So. It's a private school."

"But that's too expensive."

"Money is no object this year. Plus, don't you want the best?"

"If you say so Frank."

Mrs. O'Shea said, "Good luck boys. I'll have dinner ready when you return home."

We thanked her and went off to the College

The school seemed very big with a huge campus. But I didn't feel like I belonged there.

We then proceeded to look at Fitchburg State, Salem State and finally Bridgewater State. These schools were more in my comfort level. There was something about Bridgewater that seemed welcoming to me. I told Frank. "This is where I want to go. I like it here at Bridgewater."

"Now you're not saying that because of the money?"

"No Frank, I like it and want to go there."

Frank was very excited about my decision, especially the fact that I would be the first one in the family to go to college.

When we came home, we were greeted by Mrs. O'Shea who was very excited about our school visits. "Well how did it go boys? Did you like Boston College? Is that where you're going?"

I hated to disappoint her so I reluctantly said. "Not really. I decided on Bridgewater state. They have a good program in education and I can get my Masters there as well."

She immediately showed some disappointment in her face over my choice. She said, "What was wrong with Boston College?" She wanted me to go to a Catholic

College. Like I said, she was a very religious person, who would never miss a Sunday mass and would also go to church every day in the morning.

"I don't know Mrs. O'Shea, it just didn't seem like my kind of school."

A smile soon crossed her face. "Well, no matter. I am so happy for you. I have a little surprise for you Gregory. Come into the kitchen."

We came into the kitchen and were greeted with a cake, that said, for my college man. Congrats.

I was so touched by her thoughtfulness that I shed a few tears and hugged her. "Wow That's beautiful. Thank you."

"I'd like to see you as my adopted son, if that's okay."

"Really. And as your son, canl I you mom?"

"Of course, you can. And you Frank are my son, number two."

Frank laughed and gave her a kiss on the cheek and hugged. "I'd be proud to have you as my mother."

We sat down to have dinner that evening and then tackled the cake. She then made coffee for Frank, poured tea for herself and coco for me.

She then asked me. "Are you going to commute or stay there?"

I said. "Commute. I don't want to leave Frank.".

Frank turned to me and said. "Greg, I think it's time you get a taste of being a little more independent. You're going to live at the school."

"But Frank," I protested, "That's not for me. I want to stay home," I said defiantly.

Mrs. O'Shea then intervened. "Gregory, why don't you first give it a try. Sooner or later you'll be on your own. You can't live with your brother forever. You'll probably meet some nice girl at school, get married and raise your own family."

I laughed. "I don't think so. I've never had a date in high school and don't think it will be happening in college."

She then said. "You have to start sometime and maybe College will be the place to begin dating."

Frank just shook his head and said. "I've always encouraged him to talk to the girls in school, but he's so shy and into himself."

Mrs. O'Shea continued. "But maybe you need to find the right girl. One that you can feel comfortable with."

"I don't know.' I changed the subject and said. "I need to do my homework."

I excused myself, left the table and was going up to my room when the idea of leaving home and living with strangers was making me feel very anxious. I was half-way up the stairs when I turned around and said, "I'll do it but I'm going to need a car so I can come home on the weekends."

Frank said. "That's a no problem. I'll get a car for you."

Mrs. O'Shea said. "So why so reluctant to dorm at College?"

"Like Frank said, I'm a very shy quiet kid, who has no confidence in myself. Things became worse after my father's death."

A puzzled look appeared on her face. "But if you are so shy, why would you want to go into teaching where you'd be confronted with young children every day?"

"I know it sounds strange or doesn't make much sense but somehow that doesn't bother me. I feel like

I would have control over the situation. I would know what to expect. And Mr. Perkins is my role model. I want to be just like him."

Mrs. O'Shea looked at her watch and said. "How about that. I need to get home, after I finish these dishes."

Frank replied. "Mrs. O'Shea, go home. I'll finish cleaning up."

"Are you sure?"

"Go."

I left Mary's office again feeling good about reliving the happy days of my life.

22

PTSD

Nick had been with us for about a week without incident. Things were going pretty well with him. I mean he had his days, at times he was very anxious and had bad nightmares and problems concentrating and focusing on what he was doing. But we all have our problems, thus Larry and I were committed to accept Nick as he was. He was an Afghanistan war veteran but he never shared his war experiences with us.

It was nice to again have a new face that we could share our space with. We even talked him into playing cards with us but we couldn't convince him to eat at the shelter or even sleep there. He wanted no part of a formal institution like the shelter. In spite of his problems, I liked having him around.

I had an appointment one morning to see the doctor about my medication. He thought that I was doing so good that he wanted to wean me off it. When I came home, Larry breathlessly came running out to me. He could hardly get the words out of his mouth.

"Professor. Nick had been in a bad fight with some guys down on Washington street. I don't know if he should be staying with us. I mean he's completely out of control. It's like he is fighting the war all over again. I never saw him this bad. I don't think I want to be around him. Sure, we all have our problems but his problems are over the top. I don't know. I think we should ask him to leave."

Larry was very upset. I needed to calm him down so we could have a rationale conversation. "Slow down Larry. Let me talk to him when he gets back and then we can decide what to do. I agree, his aggression can get out of control. I'll talk to him about getting some help. You know Larry, the poor guy has had some tough experiences when he was overseas. I hate to just dump him. So, what happened Larry?"

As part of our survival, we would spend time in downtown Boston on Washington street, pan-handling for a few dollars. We always took up a position where there was a maximum of shoppers, who might give us a few dollars.

"But how did he get into a fight?"

"I assume it was over a spot where he liked to beg for coins, on Washington?

Yes, it was."

"I don't know. That doesn't make any sense. I think he gets a pension or some money from the V.A. I don't know why he would be begging for money."

Nick was one of the few people who had a steady income compared to the rest of us.

Larry and I were just about ready to go to the shelter for dinner when, Nick came through the door. He was raging drunk and yelling about some people who were after him. He could hardly walk on his own. "The bastards, they're after me. But I can outsmart them. I have my team, we'll kick the shit out of them."

I very gingerly approached him since he was so upset. I didn't know what he would do to me. "Nick. Nick. It's us, Larry and the Professor. Settle down. You're okay now. Your safe. Your back home."

Nick suddenly realized what was a happening and where he was. He then broke down and began to cry uncontrollable. "I'm sorry Professor. I'm sorry. I just thought."

When I saw the tears streaming down his face, I couldn't help but feel sorry for him. Being over Afghanistan did a number on him. I had heard about soldiers having PTSD but never actually witnessed it. Like a child that had scraped his knee and needed comforting, I held Nick in my arms. "I know Nick. No need to explain. It's your illness. Why don't you sleep here for now and we can talk about it later?"

Nick broke my embrace and began pacing around the room while shaking his head, saying. "I'm all messed up Professor. I thought I was alright but I can't get the war out of my head. It follows me everywhere I go. Dam it all, I just can't shake free from it."

"I know Nick. I know. Maybe you need to try again to see someone at the VA?"

"I can't go back to the V.A. with all those crazy people. And those doctors, they're all against me. They think I'm crazy. No. No. No. I said no."

The more he talked about the VA the more agitated he became.

I tried to calm him down as best I could but I'm not a doctor. I didn't know what to do for this poor guy.

"Okay guy settle down. No V.A.Go over there and try to sleep if off on the mat. Go."

"But if I sleep, I'll have those terrible nightmares. I'm screwed professor. Really screwed. No matter what I do."

I gently moved him down to the mat. "Just try and rest. Close your eyes and think of something pleasant, something nice."

"I don't know if I can Professor. Nothing in my life is any dam good."

"Let me try something. What was your best childhood memory? There must be one."

A smile came cascading over his face at the mention of a childhood memory. The stress and anxiety that filled his being like the water from a broken dam suddenly subsided. He smiled. "I know. The time my mother and dad took me to a fair and I got to ride on this beautiful pony. It felt like I was on top of the world. I was only five at the time."

As he was telling the story, his eyes suddenly grew weaker and he fell asleep. Peace at last.

Larry quietly said to me "See what I mean Professor? He's really bad. He scares me. I never seen anything like that before."

I tried to reassure Larry that he wouldn't hurt us although I really didn't fully believe what I was saying. We could become the enemy in his mind. "I know Larry, he can be scary. You need to realize how much emotional pain he's in. PTSD is devastating.

"What's that? PTSD?"

"It's a mental health disorder, Post traumatic Stress Disorder. He got it from being in the war. He doesn't like or rarely talk about the war."

Larry tried to understand what I was telling him. "Is it serious?"

"Very serious. When I see Mary next week, I'll talk to her about it. Maybe she can help him. I just hate to abandoned him. He's been through enough, without us telling him to get lost."

"I guess you're right Professor. You know a lot about these things." Larry than changed the subject and said. "You going to dinner at the Shelter? It's getting late"

"Not tonight. I want to keep an eye on him."

"Sure."

"But you can do me a favor and bring us back some food. Whatever you can steal."

"Will do but be careful. He's unpredictable."

Nick had a restful sleep and woke up the next morning seemingly refreshed. When I approached him, I said, "You okay Nick?"

"Yes. I feel better. No nightmares last night. Best sleep I had in a long time. Thanks, Professor, for putting up with me."

"Not a problem. You had a rough day yesterday. Do you remember what happened?"

"No. When I have these episodes, I black out. I hope I didn't hurt anyone. You know I have a short fuse on top of my illness."

He was very apologetic. "I'm sorry Professor for causing you so much grief. Usually, when I'm with some of the other homeless men, they ask me to leave. But you didn't. Why?"

"Why? Because I know what pain is about. I know what it means to suffer?"

"What do you mean?"

"Maybe I'll tell you some other time. Not now. But

I have to tell you. You scared the shit out of Larry. You need to try and keep it under control as best you can or at least try and get some help. I see a social worker at the Shelter. She's helped me a lot. I think she can help you."

"Come on Professor. No one can help me."

"That's not the right attitude. So, you don't want to go to the V.A. I think I can understand that but shit Nick, you need help. You don't want to go through life having blackouts and fighting everyone who looks at your cross-eyed or not being able to sleep because of the nightmares. Do you?"

"Of course not, I don't."

"Then give it a try. Will you at least think about it?"

Nick put his face in his hands and sighed. "I'll think about it."

23

MY THERAPY CONTINUES

That Thursday, I returned to see Mary for my counseling. I was really feeling bad for Nick but what could I do? Nothing. Except to encourage him to get help. Mary and the Doc had helped me a lot but I still wasn't ready to return home, to leave the safety and comfort of the factory, where nobody knows who you are and no one gives a dam. A place where you don't have to face your problems. Where you bury your problems in a bottle.

I knew things were beginning to change for me since I wasn't getting drunk as often and the nightmares have pretty much subsided, since the Doc put me on the medication. The real wakeup call came when my friend Mac's daughter confronted me about the pain that their father caused when he deserted their family. Their pain was clearly visible on the faces of Mac's daughters when they attended his funeral. It wasn't a pretty sight.

As I approached Mary's office, I took a deep breath before walking through her door. Mary immediately saw the worried look on my face and said, "Greg, you look like you have something on your mind. Do you want to talk about it?"

"I hesitated for a few minutes, wondering if I should bring up Nick's problems but I decided to do it. "I do. It's this new guy that moved in with me and Larry since Mac's death."

"Who is he? Does he come to the shelter?"

"No. You don't know him but he has some major problems. His name is Nick. He's a vet and has some serious PTSD."

"Why can't he go to the VA if he's a veteran?"

"No. He doesn't like the VA. Has some delusions about the place. Wants to stay away from anything associated with the V.A."

I hesitated for few seconds, before asking Mary if she would be willing to see him. "Could you see him?"

"Do you think he'd come to the shelter to see me?"

"He said he would think about it."

"Then, I'd be happy to see him. I've worked with other veterans who had similar issues."

"Thanks Mary. I really appreciate it."

"I'm only supposed to see guys in the shelter but I'm willing to make an exception for you."

"Thanks again. I know you can help him like you've helped me."

"So, things are better? The meds the doctor prescribed are helping?"

"Yes. Big improvement. Everything is good"

"Well, why don't we get back to where you left off at the last session. You were telling me about the housekeeper, you and your dad hired. Sounds like she had become more than a housekeeper. The last time we met, you were telling me about her and your decision to go to college."

I laughed. A warm feeling came across my body, just thinking about Mrs. O'Shea. "You're right. She is the mother I never had. She is a loving sweet woman who became an intricate part of our family. Mrs. O'Shea, with all her rules, made both Frank and me a better person."

"Don't you miss her Gregory? Is she still alive.?

"I miss her a lot and I really don't know what happened to her. If she's dead or alive."

"I can see that you miss her. That she means a lot to you."

"I think about her a great deal. I think about the advice she use to hand out to me, when I had a problem. Her deep faith. Her strong religion. She was a wonderful person, even thou she wanted me to go to a Catholic College."

"So, you ended up going to Bridgewater State and living there, despite you fears and concerns."

"Yes. The first year was rough on me. I hated it and wanted to come home."

"Can you tell me about it?"

"Well, like I said before, I'm a shy guy, never had any friends in High

School. Never dated. And here I was in a dorm, with three other guys who had girls in the room, making out and having sex. Drinking and getting drunk. It was a very different world than I could have ever imagined."

"How did you get along with your roommates?"

"I mean they never hassled me. Thought I was an oddball. I just didn't mix with them nor they with me. We just tolerated each other. They were not my kind of people. I couldn't wait to come home on the weekends. I pleaded with Frank to let me commute but he wouldn't allow it."

"And what about Mrs. O'Shea, your mom? What did she have to say?"

She was sympathetic but encouraged me to stick it out. She told me to try and join a club that I might be interested in. That I might find some people who are more like myself. She told me to talk to some of the other people who were in my class. Like I said, she always had the answer and always very helpful."

"So, did you follow her advice?"

"I did. I did and it worked."

"What happened?"

" I loved to write so I joined a writing club and met some nice people who shared my interests. They weren't drinkers or party animals like my roommates. We talked of trying to room together next year."

"Sounds like it worked?"

A smile came over my face. "It did. It was a small group, three guys, two girls and myself. We actually became good friends. We would go to eat together and met up in the evening to talk about our writings. Two of the guys were also going into education."

"And what about the girl in the group?"

She was pretty and real nice. I initially had trouble relating to her but she made me feel so comfortable that talking to her was no longer a problem. It felt good to be able to talk to a girl. Real nice. Something that I had never experienced in all my years in school. I began spending less time going home and spending more time with my new friends. I had even invited them home. They loved my brother Frank and fell in love with, Mrs. O'Shea, especially her cooking."

"That was a big change in your life. To be able to socialize and even talk to a girl."

I laughed. "It was. I was so happy."

"I assume that the rest of your first year was good?"

"I couldn't begin to explain how happy I was. All the fears and anxieties I had, completely vanished."

Mary looked at her watch and noticed that we had gone over our time. "Gregory, it looks like our time is up. This was a good session. See you next week?"

"Absolutely. And what about Nick?"

"When you come next time, bring him along and let me meet him. Let's see if we can ease him into it. Okay?"

"Thanks. You're the best."

"You have a good evening Gregory."

When Larry and I returned to the factory, I told Nick that Mary was willing to see him.

"I don't know Professor. I still want to think about it."

"Nick, she just wants to meet you. That's all."

He reluctantly agreed to meet her. "I guess just to meet her will be okay."

It was a beginning for Nick.

24

NICK

On the following weekend, I was playing cards with Nick in the afternoon. Larry went into downtown Boston, looking to see if he could beg for some money since he was getting very low on coins.

As we were playing cards, Nick asked me how I ended up homeless especially since I was a bright intelligent guy. He didn't believe I fit the profile of a homeless person. Nick said, "I don't understand how it could happen to someone like you."

"I don't know Nick, if there is only one profile of a homeless person. Anyone could become homeless for a whole myriad of reasons." I told him a little about myself but not the whole story. I than turned to him and asked. "So, Nick, what's your story?"

Nick was initially reluctant to talk but finally he said. "That's fair enough Professor. Let's see. Where do I begin? I was raised by my mom after my father deserted our family. I was only 10 years old when it happened. I was completely devastated. Never saw it coming. I mean, I got along pretty good with the old man. When he left, I went berserk? Crazy. I just didn't understand why he left me. While Nick related his story, a question kept running through my head. *Why did I leave home? Why?* Nick continued to related his story. "My mother later told me that he was involved with a younger woman, a woman who later left him. I couldn't stop smiling when I heard about my dad being dumped. When I found out about his girlfriend leaving him, I thought he more than deserved it.

My mom struggled financially. She didn't have any definable skills thus she ended up working her ass off as a nurse's aide in a nursing home.

My father later disappeared from our life. He never gave us one single cent for child support. I really felt bad for my mom. When I was old enough to get a job, I worked at the local Stop and Shop, stocking shelves. After High school, mom wanted me to go to college. But I didn't want to be a burden on her. She had no money. Plus, I didn't do too well in school. I was far from a bright star. I spent a lot of time in detention."

"Why detention?"

"Mostly for fighting or failing to do my assignments."

"Looks like you always had a shot temper?"

"Just got worse after the military."

"What about dating? Did you ever date in High school?"

"Not really. Girls never interested me."

"What did you do after graduation?"

"After High School, I worked in construction for a few years until I got into a fight with the boss. I was fired. Like I said, I always had a short fuse. I than tried working as a mechanic with a high school friend of mine. The work was dirty and not very satisfying. I wasn't cut out to be an auto mechanic. After 2 years I left that job. By then, my options were becoming limited. I didn't know what I wanted or where I was going, so I decided to join the Marines. I was 22 years old. I thought that maybe I could find my way in the service, maybe make a career of it."

"How did the Marines work out for you?"

"Somehow, the Marines was a good fit for me, at least initially. The service provided an outlet for my aggression. I got paid for being aggressive."

I was sent oversees to Afghanistan for my first tour of duty. I loved the action and the guys I was with. Many of them were like me, trying to figure out what to do with their lives. What could be better? Free room and board. I was also able to send most of my paycheck home to my mother.

Then everything turned to shit, which is the story of my life. At 28, I got news from home, that my mother was suffering from cancer. Just like her. Always trying to protect me. She never told me about it since she didn't want to worry me. Imagine that, she didn't want to worry me. She died." Nick went silent for a few seconds. I could see the tears cascading down his cheeks. This tough guy, a fighter was crying. "I was able to get leave to attend her funeral. Her death took everything out of me. She was the only person in my life that mattered and now she was dead. I started to do more drinking but not enough to interfere with my work.

I returned to my unit and was promoted to Sargent and was put in charge of a unit. These were my men and I took the responsibility seriously. I eventually returned to Afghanistan, and after a year it happened. Me along with my crew were out on recon when our vehicle hit a landmine. I was tossed 10 feet out of the Hum-V." He paused for a few seconds, while his hands began to tremble. "All my men were killed. I sustained a broken leg and arm when I landed on my side. Several pieces of shrapnel found their way into my head." He showed me the scar. "I failed my men. My job was to protect them and I didn't. I will always carry the guilt of their deaths. To this day it still haunts me. I couldn't help but thinking how guilt can be so burdensome and destructive.

I ended up in a GI hospital and later was discharged to a psychiatric facility because of my diagnosis, PTSD. I was a mess. I soon was discharged from the Marines and was sent to a VA facility because of my illness. One day I decided that I had enough of the VA. I had enough of everything. I left the hospital, with a VA pension of 100% for my injuries. Now, once a month I go to the bank to collect my blood money and drink it."

"I couldn't begin to understand what happened to you Nick. I am so sorry Nick, for all that you have been through. That's a lot for one man to carry. But your story sounds similar to many of us. We all carry with us the burden of guilt for something we didn't do or should have done. But now I'm just beginning to be-lieve that this road of homelessness and despair is not the road I want to travel. It's more than a dead end, it's a death sentence."

"Your right Professor, it is a death sentence. A death sentence that is well deserved."

And with those words he left the building.

25

JOAN

I was about ready to leave for my appointment with Mary and asked Nick to come with me. "Nick. You said you agreed to meet my therapist Mary. Let's go."

When Nick hesitated for a few seconds, I knew he was reluctant to see her. "I thought about it Professor and decided that I don't want to do it. Sorry. Therapy isn't my thing. They tried it with me when I was at the hospital. No good."

I raised my voice and said. "That's bullshit. Come on Nick. All I'm asking is that you meet her. Just meet her."

I began to think, why would somebody be so reluctant to get help. Maybe they didn't want to look at who they really are and what they had done.

"I can't do it."

I hated to threaten him but it was the only thing I could do. "Nick, do you like being with us?"

"Of course, I do. What a silly question."

"Either you come to meet her or you can find somewhere else to hang out."

Nick shook his head. He really came to enjoy our company, especially me. He hesitated for a few seconds before saying. "You're a tough guy to deal with my friend."

"Yes I am. I just care about you. You're a good guy. I hate to see you waste your life."

"Okay my friend but only to meet her. We good?"

"We're good."

We than headed for the shelter. Once we entered the building, I said. "See Nick, this is the shelter where we sleep and get our meals. Not too bad?"

"Great. Looks good. I just don't like being in closed space. That's probably why I didn't stay at the V.A."

"Okay. Let's go and see Mary. I think you'll like her."

"Now it's just to meet her? Right? No therapy."

I reassured him that it would be just a brief meeting. "You got it pal. Just to meet her. Nothing more."

When we went to the office. I gently knocked on the door. Mary came to the door and said, "Hi, won't you step in and take a seat?"

Nick quickly said, "No. No. Just want to say hello and then I have to leave."

Mary didn't force him to come in and quietly said "Hello, my name is Mary. I'm the social worker at the shelter. You must be Nick?"

She extended her hand and he took it, saying, "Pleasure to meet you I need to go." He quickly exited the office, feeling he had met my demand.

"Okay Nick. Hope to see you again."

Before she could get the words out of her mouth. Nick was down the hallway and out the door.

I began yelling at him. "Nick. Come on back. Nick."

Mary in her always understanding ways said. "Gregory. It's Okay. When he's ready, he'll come back."

I just shook my head, not responding to her and took a seat in her office.

"Gregory, let's just focus on you for now. Okay?

I shook my head and said. "Sure."

"Now the last time we got together, you told me about meeting new friends and that your college experience was better than you thought it would be. Is that right?"

"Yes. It was completely different than I thought it would be? I liked my new friends and I really enjoyed my classes."

"You said that there were two young women in your group. Tell me about your relationships with them."

I laughed. "They were just good friends. I never dated them. We would just socialize as a group. So, you never dated in College?"

"I never dated until I met my wife Joan."

"Tell me about meeting your wife."

"Let's see. Where do I begin? My wife and I were both majoring in education thus we shared some of the same classes. I had noticed her on many occasions. I thought to myself, *I would give anything to talk to her, to have a date with her.* I was immediately attracted to Joan. She was beautiful, energetic and had a good sense of humor. I wanted to start a conversation with her on many occasions but was afraid she would reject me. I was very awkward when it came to girls. I never dreamed she would ever date me.

This particular class I was in with her, the Professor assigned a project. He would pair up two students to work together. Would you believe it? He had chosen me to work with Joan. She was my partner. I mean, what a stroke of luck. I couldn't believe it."

"So, what happened when you met her for the first time?"

"I was dumbstruck. I had trouble looking at her

and the words seemed to get stuck in my throat when I tried to talk to her. It was like I had lost my voice and couldn't speak. Thankfully, she initiated the conversation. by introducing herself to me.

Cheerfully she began, "Hi, my name is Joan Kelley. I guess we'll be working together on this project?"

I didn't respond. I couldn't answer. My mouth just wouldn't work.

She finally said. "Hello in there? What's your name? You're going to have to talk to me or we'll never be able to complete this project. I know you can you speak."

I apologized for not responding to her and hesitated before saying. "My name is Gregory?"

"Nice to meet you. What do they call you?"

"Greg would do fine. And you?"

"Just Joan. Plain Joan? You know like a plain Jane."

But she was far from a plain Jane or Joan.

She immediately began to talk about the project. "I thought we could divide up the work and then compare notes by meeting in the library. What do you think Greg? If that's alright with you?"

It was so nice to hear her call my name. "Sure Joan. That sounds great." I wouldn't dare say no. I couldn't.

She than looked quizzically at me. "You seem very nervous Greg. Believe me I don't bite and I'm a nice young woman."

I laughed and said, "I tend to be on shy side."

"Really. No girlfriends?"

I laughed, "No girlfriends."

"Oh, that's so sad Greg. Well, now that you're in college, things might change for you."

And so, began our relationship.

26

TROUBLE AGAIN

One evening, I and Larry went to the shelter to spend the night. The sleeping quarters mimicked an Army barracks with cots on each side of the isle in a large room. Larry's bunk was next to mine. It must have been about three in the morning, when I was awoken by Larry who seemed to be having a bad dream. I'm a light sleeper to begin with so I was easily awoken by him. I got out of my bunk and shook him saying. "Larry. Larry. Wake up you're having a bad dream"

Larry awoke, and was sweating profusely. He was in a state of panic.

I shook him and said. "Larry wake-up. You're having a bad dream."

"Yes. Worse than any bad dream I ever had."

"What were you dreaming?"

"I dreamt about my mother. I haven't dreamt about her since leaving home."

"So, what was so bad about that?"

"I dreamt that she was badly hurting. She was near

death laying on the floor because of her dinking. Like the booze finally got to her."

"But it's just a dream Larry."

"No, It's not. It's an omen. I need to get to her and save her. She needs me."

"But Larry, It's just a dream. Trust me."

Larry started to put on his pants. "I've got to go."

"But it's the middle of the night."

"You don't understand. I've got to go. She's my mother."

"Listen Larry. Wait until morning and I'll go with you. Okay?"

He hesitated for a few second before agreeing to remain at the shelter until morning.

The next morning, Larry woke me up at 6:00am and said. "Let's get going."

I was still half asleep. "Shit Larry, I'm not even awake yet. It's been years since you've seen her. Can't you wait for a few more minutes? I need to get some breakfast and take a shower. Do you even know where she lives?"

"I think she still lives in Allston. That's where she was the last time, I saw her."

"At least it's not very far from here. We can take public transportation."

Larry's anxiety heightened. He didn't bother to shower or grab something to eat. He just kept pacing around the dining room. The other men started yelling at him to sit down. He reacted by leaving the building and waited for me outside.

When I finally was ready to go, it was 7:00am. Just our luck, the rain was pouring outside. I must admit, that I was somewhat fearful on going to his mother's apartment. From what he said, there were a lot of sketchy characters where she lived. Not the best clientele for a street walking prostitute, his mother We took the subway and the trolley to Allston. By the time we got there, it was about 8:00am. It was a rundown neighborhood with burnt out cars. All kinds of graffiti on vacant buildings. Broken windows. People sleeping in doorways. Rubbish covered the street. It was not very inviting.

We were walking about fifteen minutes while Larry was trying to remember the address of his mother's apartment.

I was becoming frustrated and finally said. "Larry, are you sure this is the street?"

"I'm pretty sure." He kept straining his neck, and examining every building, looking for a familiar landmark. "I know it's here Professor."

Finally, he became all excited, and began yelling. "Professor, there it is. There it is. See that brown stone building?"

I replied, "The one where the shingles are falling of the sides off the building?" That one?"

"That's the one. We live on the top floor."

Larry was right. Her apartment was on the fourth floor. We rang the bell but nobody answered. It really didn't matter because the front lock was broken. Anyone could easily access the building.

When we entered the entry way, we were confronted with a homeless man sleeping peacefully in the corner of the hallway.

We quietly passed him bye and proceeded to make the long trek up the flight of stairs which were covered with debris and dust. I bet the place hadn't been cleaned for years.

The first thing that affronted my senses was the smell of booze and urine. It looked like the corners of the floors were a convenient place for a person to relieve themselves.

Breathlessly, we reached the top floor which had three apartments. Larry began to knock feverishly on each of the door yelling, "mommy, mommy. It's me Larry. You okay."

No answer. His anxiety began to escalate. He continued to yell, which drew the complaints of neighbors, who yelled back at him. "Shut up. Don't you know what time it is?"

I turned to Larry and said. "Larry, maybe she's not home."

"Not home? She seldom goes out before noon. I know she's in there." He again began to panic. I could clearly here it in his voice.

"All right Larry settle down. Let me see if I can pick the lock. It doesn't look very secure." I took my pen knife out of my pocket and was able to open the door.

Larry immediately rushed into the room and was confronted with an empty living room. He then rushed into the bedroom, where he found his mother, half clothed, lying across the bed with an empty bottle of whiskey next to her side.

It was beyond my comprehension. Why did he want to return to a whoring alcoholic, who didn't give a shit about him? But I guess, the young child in him, wants and keeps trying to obtain the love of one's parent, no matter how badly that parent treats you. A mother is a mother. The bond that separates a mother and child can never be broken, no matter how hard we try. No matter how badly a mother treats that child. But I admit, my bitch of a mother is the exception. There was never a bond between her and me.

Larry frantically began shaking her and yelling "Mommy. Mommy? Get up. Look, it's your son, Larry?"

Eventually she was shaken out of her unconsciousness. And said, "Who the hell are you?"

Larry was behaving like a little kid, who wanted his mommy to love him. "Mommy it's me Larry, you're son."

She responded to her son in a cruel and biting manner. "What the hell are you doing here? Get out. Get out. I don't want to see you. You little shit. You deserted me. Why did you come back now? You need money? Well I don't have any."

"I don't want money. I was worried about you mommy. I thought something happened. I had a terrible feeling. I had a dream that you were hurt, that's why I came. I know I should have come sooner but...."

She interrupted him. "But my ass. You were always a nuisance. You were a mistake." She started to yell. "Do you hear me, a mistake and the bastard who brought you into the world didn't even pay me a dime. You should have never left your poor mother. What kind of a son are you? You fuckin moron."

At this point Larry was in tears pleading with his mother. "I know I'm not a good son. I'm sorry mom. I'm sorry."

"You little wimp. If you want to do something useful, get me the bottle of gin on the table, your useless bastard"

"But mom, that's not good for you. It will kill you."

"I don't give a shit. Get out of my house." She got up

from her bed and started throwing things at him. The phone and the clock.

I grabbed Larry by the arm and said, "Time to go. Larry let's get out of here. Things haven't change."

As I was pulling Larry through the door he again began to cry and frantically yelling "Mommy. Mommy."

My heart was hurting for him. The poor kid. I could not believe that a mother could treat her son that way. It was bad.

We took the bus back to the factory. Larry was complete broken. Again, deserted by his mother. Rejected by his mother. When we returned to the factory, he immediately went for his bottle and drank himself asleep.

How ironic, that he should turn to the bottle like his mother. I guess he learned from his mother to solve his problems by drinking.

27

THERAPY

The following week I returned to meet with Mary. I was feeling depressed over what happened to my good friend Larry. He is a good kid who went through hell with his drunken whore of a mother. I could relate to his situation since my mother was far from the mother of the year. I was so upset about Larry that I didn't even bother to bug Nick about returning to see my social worker. I had enough on my plate to deal with never mind Nick.

When I walked through the door of Mary's office, she immediately saw the grim disappointment and painful look on my face. Mary was very good on picking up on my feeling states.

"Gregory, you look like you again had a bad week?"

I stood silent for a few seconds, trying to gather my thoughts. I finally said. "I don't know Mary. I think I'm going to leave the factory. I can't take the problems of my friends any more. I have enough problems of my own without taking on other people's. I need to focus on myself. I just can't take it anymore, I just can't."

"So, tell me what you're so fed up about? Is it Nick again?"

I shook my head and said. "No, Larry, my other friend." I related to her what happened with Larry when we found his mother.

"What's going on Greg? Why are you feeling so involved about people you hardly know?"

I became angry with her, since these people had become my support system and my only friends, no matter how screwed up they are and they are screwed up. 'You're the social worker. You tell me?"

"Maybe it's a question you need to ask yourself Gregory? Maybe it's somehow related to your own problems."

Mary's response and her unwillingness to answer my question caused me to become angrier. "What the hell are you talking about Mary? I had good father and...." Then I stopped before completing my sentence.

"Continue Greg."

"Forget it. Mary. Let's get on with my work."

"How can we get on Gregory? It seems like Larry's problem hit a nerve with you. Maybe it has to do with your own mother, who you feel was not a mother. Or whatever happened in your own family that led you to leave them?"

Mary's comments and questions stopped me cold. She was right. But did I really want to talk about the family I left. "Wow Mary. You don't pull any punches. I sure as hell didn't have any feelings for that bitch, my own mother, who was never my mother. And, I again hesitated before continuing my thoughts. Painful thoughts that I didn't want to talk about. "I haven't been a good father. Haven't been a good husband..." Before I could finish the sentence, I started to cry.

"These men seem to be bringing up many of your own unresolved issues. Once we work through these issues, I think you won't become so upset with your friends. I don't think you need to leave your friends unless you really want to. But you certainly don't have to take on their problems. Like yourself, help is available to them if they want it. Getting help is their decision."

"I guess You're right. I just wanted to do something."

"Gregory, you clearly are a good man. I can see that. Now you have to believe in your own goodness."

"I hope so. For now, I'd like to pick-up where we left off. Is that okay?"

"Whatever you say. The last time we talked, you mentioned how you first met your wife to be."

"Yes. It was one of the best years of my life."

"Why don't you begin by telling me her name again."

"Joan. Joan Kelley. When I first saw her, I couldn't believe how beautiful she is."

"Can you describe her to me?"

"Yes, I will never forget her. She is about five feet five inches. Her eyes are like the stars in the sky. They sparkled when she talks. A very outgoing person. Loves all kinds of music. Has no problem holding a conversation. She speaks her mind but is also sensitive about what she says and tries not to offend people. A great sense of humor.

"Wow. I can see that you were very taken by her, like you found the perfect woman."

"She is perfection and I miss her. I was so excited to work on this project with her. We met about twice a week. I only wished it was four times a week.

I found out that she came from a big family, which was quite different then my family, of Frank and I. She was the oldest of five brothers and sister. Three of them were in high school and the last sibling was a girl named Margaret who was in middle school. A loving family. Her mother was a teacher and her father worked as a salesman for Sears in Boston.

We worked together on the project very well. You know what I mean, we clicked. I finally got up the courage to ask her for a date after we had been working together for three weeks. The project was coming to an end

I said to her. "Well Joan, we're almost finished with the project. I have to say, I enjoyed working with you. I guess the only thing we need to decide on is the presentation. I was thinking that you would do a better job at presenting than me. You know, I'm a bit on the shy side. Would you mind presenting to the class?"

She looked at me as if to say what are you talking about. "I don't mind doing it Greg but this is a joint project. We both need to do it."

My breathing suddenly became labored at the thought of presenting to some thirty people. I began to stutter. "I don't know..., Joan. I don't.. know if I could do it."

Joan became very emphatic about my situation. But she was not going to take no for an answer. "Gregory, I know you're shy and nervous. That's clearly evident but its' time to get over it. You're a bright intelligent person. You'll do fine. I know you can do it. I have all the confidence in the world in you."

It was hard during those early days to say no to Joan, especially after she showered me with all those compliments.

I finally said "Okay. I'll do it, together."

"Great Greg. We're going to hit a homerun, knock the ball out of the park."

And then it was time for me to ask her out. This was worse than presenting to a classroom of thirty people. Joan got up from her seat at the library, collected her books and papers started to make her way towards the door. I finally yelled. "Joan. Excuse me Joan. I have something to ask you."

She quickly turned around and began to walk towards me saying, "I hope your still going to present?"

"No. No. I'm still going to do it."

"So, what's up Mr. Gregory?"

"I was wondering if you'd like to go to the movies, maybe this Saturday. If you don't want to go, that's alright. I was just thinking it might be...."

Before I could finish my rambling proposal for a date she said. "Gregory Stop. Stop. Stop all the talking. For Heaven's sake. I'd love to go out with you."

I was utterly surprised. Completely dumbfounded. I certainly thought she would say no. "You would?"

"Gregory, do you have a hearing problem? I said yes. Now I have to run to my next class."

"Before you leave, what kind of movies do you like?"

"Anything but horror movies. You know the kind. Slice and dice."

"What about Science fiction? They say the new movie, The Empire Strikes Back is pretty good."

She made a face. "Science Fiction is okay but not my favorite kind of movie. What about comedies?"

"I love comedies. How about seeing The Blues Brothers?"

"Now you're talking Gregory. Let's do it."

She was about to walk out the door when I again yelled. "Joan. Joan stop."

She turned around in disgust as did everyone else who was in the library at my yelling. "What now Gregory? I said yes. We'll see the Blues Brothers. So, what else?"

"I know you did but I don't know where you live and I don't have your telephone number."

She laughed loudly, the laugh I came to love. An infectious laugh. "Sorry Gregory. How stupid of me."

I immediately came to her defense. "O no, you're far from stupid. You're brilliant."

"Believe me Gregory. That was stupid." She took out her notebook and wrote the address and phone number on a piece of paper and handed it to me.

"Thanks Joan."

"Okay, see you this Saturday. Give me a call and let me know when the movie starts?"

"Will do. Perfect. I'll give you a call."

When I went home on Friday, I couldn't wait to tell my brother about her. I was walking on air. I was going on a date with the women of my dreams, my very first date. I needed to pinch myself to make sure I wasn't dreaming. I was in a complete state of disbelief.

28

BIG BROTHER LENDS A HAND

Friday night I came home early from school since my last class was at 4:00pm. I put my key in the door and opened it. I was whistling which is something I never do. Completely out of character.

I walked into the kitchen with a broad smile on my face where Mrs. O'Shea was preparing her specialty, which I loved, Corned beef and cabbage. The aroma of her cooking filled my nostrils which danced with delight. I immediately gave her a kiss and said. "Good evening my favorite cook and the woman of all ages."

I than began to dance around the kitchen floor with her.

She began to laugh and said, "Well its looks like you had a good day today. You must have done well on your exams. I never saw you act like this before."

"Better than that mom." We now called her mom rather than Mrs. O'Shea. "I found the girl of my dreams. I'm in love. Really in love."

Mrs. O'Shea shook her head and laughed. "You're in love? Really in love?"

She had a puzzled look on her face. "What happened?"

"I met this wonderful girl when the professor assigned us to do a project together. I tell you Mom, it was a gift from heaven."

"Slow down young man. Tell me about her."

"Mom, she's a beautiful, intelligent woman who accepted my invitation to go on a date. Can you believe it? She said yes."

"You mean this is your first date with her and you're acting like a crazy man?"

"Yes. Yes, I'm crazy in love." I than yelled. "Isn't it wonderful?"

"Greg settle down, it's 'only your first date. How can you can't be in love?"

"But your wrong mom, I'm in love. You know? Love at first site. Right?"

I than went up to my room and changed my clothes and got rid of my books and papers.

One hour later my brother Frank came through the door. He took off his shoes before entering the living the room as instructed by Mrs. O'Shea, our mom.

He shook his heads in disgust, saying, "What a day. I'm glad that it's over. So many things went wrong. The shipment of lumber arrived late. One of the saws malfunctioned. What could go wrong, went wrong. Hope tomorrow is better."

When I came down from upstairs and entered the kitchen, I saw my brother and said." "Hi Frank. Good to see you."

When Frank saw me smiling, he said. "What are you smiling about? I hope you're still doing well in school?"

With full confidence I said. "I've got the grades

covered brother. Better then school, I have a date this Saturday."

Frank had a puzzled look on his face. "What do you mean a date? Like with a girl?"

"Come on Frank, of course a girl."

It was liked someone poured a bucket of sunshine over him. His gloomy face faded away and it was replaced with a happy smile. He came over and hugged me. "That's terrific Greg. I'm so happy for you. A date? Wow, college is doing you a lot of good. You have to tell me all about her at dinner. Let me get cleaned up. He turned around to face Mrs. O'Shea and said. "Do I smell, what I think I smell?"

Mrs. O'Shea with pride said. "You certainly do. I thought I'd give you boys a treat tonight by making your favorite meal."

Frank, went over and hugged and kissed her on the cheeks. "You're the best mom."

With disgust she said. "Look what you did Frank. Covered me face with all that grease and grime."

"Makes no difference mom. You're still the most beautiful woman on the planet."

"Enough of your blarney. Get cleaned up. But I have to admit, I love you boys just as if you were my own flesh and blood."

During the meal, I told Frank all about Joan and he was very happy for me. I was always like the little boy who would turn red even when he looked at a girl.

Frank over the years had become my second father. I could always depend on him to support me, give me courage and provide me with life experience.

After dinner I said, "Frank, could I talk to you in private, alone?"

Mrs. O'Shea laughed. "I think I know what this is all about. I'll let you two off the hook today and do the dish myself. But only for tonight. You men have some important business to discuss and I think it has to do with Gregory's new-found love," she said with a Cheshire smile on her face.

We left the kitchen and went into the living room. Once we were both comfortable seated, I turned to Frank and said. "Frank. What do I do? I never was on a date before and she's a knock out. I can't even believe that she wants to go out with me. I don't know what to say or how to act."

With the approach of a businessman, he said, "To begin with, where are you going?"

"To the movies. We're going to see the Blues Brothers."

"Good choice. Can't get into any trouble with a comedy. Now, the first thing you have to do on a date is relax. Remember, she's only human. You might think she's Venus De Malo, but she's just another girl. Nothing to be scared of."

I laughed. "That's easy for you to say. You've had plenty of dates."

"True but remember, first date or last date it's all the same. Don't put on an act. Be yourself. Don't try to be something you're not. Ask questions about her. That will show her, you care. Women love that stuff. Keep the conversation going. If you can't think of something, just talk about school, or the weather or sports. Got it?"

"I think so? I have to tell you Frank, this is very helpful. I'm feeling relaxed already"

"That's good Greg."

"Now, what do I do after the movie?"

"Go for a pizza or something. Like Jimmy's Pizza Palace. Not too far from the theatre."

"And then what?"

"And then what? You have to be kidding Greg. You really don't know what to do"

"That's why I wanted to talk to you."

"Okay. Another thing that the ladies like, is a guy with good manners. A guy who's polite. Open and close the door. When you go to the Pizza place, pull out her chair."

"Now here's the tough one for me Frank. When I take her home, what do I do at the end of the night?"

"Don't be overly aggressive."

I laughed. "That I can handle."

"Begin by testing the waters. Hold her hand as you walk her to do the door."

"What if she takes her hand away?"

"The end. The romance is over."

"If she takes my hand, then what?"

"Here comes the good stuff. Gently kiss her on the lips. Nothing to passionate. It's the first date. If she likes it, you'll know. She might even kiss you back.

"That's it?"

"Future dates will take care of themselves, if she likes you and I know she will. You're a good sincere, honest kid. I'm so happy for you Greg. You deserve the best and she sounds like a wonderful person. Well, I have an early day tomorrow. I need to go to bed. We can talk again tomorrow, my little brother."

"Thanks Frank. I really appreciate your talking to me and helping me out. I feel much better now."

"That's what big brothers are for."

Mary then said. "Sounds like you brother Frank

was more like a father than a brother. A real big help to you."

"Yes. Like I said, he was always there when I needed him. I couldn't live without him."

"That's what I don't understand Gregory. You left behind all that love and caring you got from your brother and your new mom, Mrs. O'Shea and your wife and child to become homeless?" It doesn't make sense."

I shook my head. "I now it doesn't. I don't know if I really understood what I gave up. When I hear myself talk, it doesn't make sense? That's why I need to figure it out. That's why I'm coming to see you. To find a way back to the life I had. And I also need to get rid of this guilt I've been carrying around for all these years. A guilt that clouds all my thinking. A guilt that caused me to run away."

"And you will Gregory. You will. I see our time is up. I think we're making some progress. See you next week?"

"I would never miss a session. Thanks Mary."

"You are more than welcome. And remember what we said about your friends. You can't make them change. They have to want it themselves. You need to learn to accept people as they are."

I left this session with more questions than answers about myself and my life but like Mary said, It's a good start."

29

THE DESIRE FOR CHANGE

When I returned to the factory from having breakfast at the shelter, I walked into our place and saw Nick sitting in a corner of the room playing solitaire while Larry was just finishing a bottle of cheap wine, he bought with his panhandling money. It was about 9:30 a.m. on that Friday morning in November. The wind was howling and they were forecasting snow for tonight. Larry had stopped coming to eat and sleep at the shelter since visiting his mother. When I saw him sitting on the floor with his dirty and torn clothes and a bottle of wine between his legs, I just shook my head. I remembered what Mary had told me about Larry and Nick. They weren't my problem. It was up to them to do something about their lives. In spite of what she said, I couldn't help but feel badly for Larry, a young man, who had his whole life ahead of himself. I desperately wanted to ignore him, but my bleeding heart wouldn't allow me to do it.

Once inside our space, I dropped a bag full of food on the table and said. "If you guys want to eat, I've got a bag full of goodies from the shelter. The cook, Hank, gave me some good stuff. He's an interesting guy who use to be homeless and now he's working as a chef at an uptown restaurant. As you know, he periodically volunteers his time to cooks at the shelter. He made it. So, can you. He gave me this food as a favor. You two guys don't have to stay homeless"

Nick completely ignored my comments about the cook. Instead, he immediately dropped his deck of cards on the floor and said. "Thanks Professor. I could use a bite to eat. Starved. You know professor, you're a good guy. Always thinking of us. Always trying to help us. I appreciate it.

"You're welcome."

He then chuckled and had a silly grin on his face. "No lecture today Professor about getting help?"

"No lecture Nick. Not any more I decided that it was up to you not me. If you want to live a shitty existence, that's up to you."

"I like that. Like what you said. It is up to me. Maybe someday I'll try to improve myself but not today. Sarcastically he said to Larry. "Right Larry. Right now, we like our shitty life."

Larry didn't answer him or even get up for the food. He just sat in the corner, staring into space with a blank expression on his face.

I went over and poked him in the arm and said. "Larry the man is talking to you. Is this the kind of life you want, a shitty one?"

I repeated it again but got now answer. "I than became angry with him. "Shit Larry, say something will you." I seldom would get angry with him but I was feeling frustrated.

Larry finally responded. "What the hell do you want me to say professor. I don't know who my father is. I have a mother, if you want to call her that, who doesn't want me in her life. Yes. My life is shitty. What kind of a mother rejects her own child? Treat me like dirt. Allowed me to get beat up by her pimp. What else can it be? I am a nobody. A piece of disposable garbage."

"But you're not Larry. You're a good person. I know that. So, doesn't Nick. It's your mother who is garbage, not you. Remember I also had a mother who rejected me, since I got in the way of her career. But I'm doing something about it. Like I said to Nick, I'm not going to force you to do anything. It's up to you. At least have something to eat. The both of you should come to the shelter tonight. The temperature is going to drop. If you don't come with me, they'll find you tomorrow frozen like popsicles."

Larry didn't say a word but Nick quickly replied. "Don't worry my friend. We can get warm with the rest of the crew that live here. They always have a fire going. You know."

"Yes, I know that one of these days I'm going to find the both of you dead. That's' what I know."

As I left the building and walked into the cold of the evening Nick laughed.

Like Mary said. It's their life. I can't do any more to save them. I did my best.

As I walked down the street towards the shelter a cold wind chilled my fragile body. The wind lifted the papers and garbage that littered the street. The swirling wind and papers looked like a mini tornado. It reminded me of the men at the shelter, their lives were like the garbage caught up in the wind, just swirling aimlessly around.

30

THE DATE

I continued my sessions with Mary, which I had come to look forward to.

It was the first week in December. After I sat down in front of her desk, Mary said. "Can I get you a cup of coffee or something to drink?"

Mary always had a coffee pot brewing in her office. Since the air had chilled my body, I quickly and thankfully responded to her offer. "Wow, that sounds good. I'd like a cup."

"Cream and sugar?

"Just make it black." I drank my coffee which felt good going down my throat and it warmed my insides. She then took her seat behind her desk.

"Thank you, Mary. I needed that."

"You're more than welcome Greg. Tell me, how's it going with your friends at the factory?"

"I took your advice and accepted the fact that they are not ready to change. I have continuously tried to convince them to at least come to the shelter since the weather has turned really cold but they wouldn't listen to me." I shrugged my shoulders. "What can you do?"

"You're right Gregory. You can't do anything but I can see by looking into your eyes that you're both frustrated and sad about their decisions."

"Of course, I am, they're my friends. But I guess I'll have to learn to live with it."

"Yes, that's right. Gregory your concern for them tells me that you are a good sensitive guy that cares about people."

"I don't know about that. You still don't know everything about me. You might change your mind when you hear my whole story. I'm not such a wonderful guy."

"Let me be the judge of that. I think it's time to get back to where you left off, when I last saw you. You started to tell me about your first date, with your wife. So, how did it go?"

A smile came over my face at the memory of my first date with Joan. "It went really well. She lived in Waltham with her parents and four siblings. I can't begin to tell you how nervous I was, going to pick her up. When I walked through the door I was greeted by the whole family. Initially the words started to stick in my throat. I could hardly speak but Joan and her family made me feel very comfortable. They asked me about my family and I'm told them I lived with my brother Frank but I didn't go into any details about my mom or my father. They accepted my answer and didn't' try to push me for more information.

Their house was a modest three bed room ranch, which was nicely decorated. Pictures of the children graced the wall along with a bridal picture of her parents. The house had a nice warm welcoming feeling to it.

We stayed at her house for about thirty minutes before leaving for the movies.

When we got to the theater in Waltham, we both enjoyed the movie along with a box of popcorn. It felt good to laugh, especially with Joan.

Following the movie, we went for pizza and some soft drinks as planned.

At the Pizzeria, I immediately felt relaxed enough to begin a conversation with her, which surprised me. Everything seemed to be going as my brother Frank had predicted.

I began by saying, "So, what did you think about the movie?"

"I loved it. It was a welcomed change from all the homework and school."

"I feel the same way. Seems like you enjoy comedies?"

"I love them. Tell you why. It's a welcome relief from all the trouble and violence in the world. Comedies help me to forget.

"They are a nice change of pace but my favorite kind of movies are horror movies."

She laughed. "Horror movies? You have to be kidding me. Really?"

"Come on Joan. Don't laugh at me. I get a kick out of them. I certainly don't take them seriously. It's just another way to escape the bad happenings in this crazy world of ours. For you its comedy and for me it's horror." She began to laugh, a laugh I fell in love with. "You are a hoot Gregory."

What do you listen to for music Greg? Don't tell me, heavy metal."

"No. That's not for me"

"Thank God. So, what do you like?"

"I love Jazz like Jerry Mulligan, Louis Armstrong, Billie Holiday, Nina Simone. Those people."

"I have to say, I never really had a chance to listen to any kind of Jazz."

I than became excited at a chance for another date. "Well, maybe someday, I can take you to a Jazz club."

"I'd love it."

"And what about you? What kind of music do you like?

"Me? I like pop. Artists such as Billy Joel, Olivia Newton John, Diana Ross. People like that. Do you ever listen to any other kind of music aside from Jazz?"

"O, sure. As a matter of fact, I like all those artists you mentioned. One of my favorites songs is The Pina Colada Song and Queen's Crazy Little Thing Called love."

Her face lit up when I mentioned those songs. We made a real connection. "I love those songs myself. Good to hear we have some common ground. How about politics? You into politics?"

I really didn't want to answer that questions since I didn't know what political party she belonged to and I didn't want to get into a disagreement. Plus, I had little time or interest in politics. Events of my life and struggling to get bye consumed all of my time like a hungry bear. So, I didn't offer her much to her question, except to say. "I, along with my family are democrats but to tell the truth, I never had developed much of an interest in politics."

Joan seemed surprised by my answer and jokingly admonished me. "Greg, I'm ashamed of you. Politics is what makes the world go around. You need to get involvement. It affects our life and who we are."

Her comments made my face turn red with embarrassment. I began to stutter. "I. huh. I... don't know what to say."

She than realized how uncomfortable her comments had made me and apologized. "I'm so sorry Greg. I didn't mean to embarrass you. Please forgive me? It's just that I'm very passionate about what's happening in the world, politically. I need to learn to restrain my passion when it comes to politics."

"Not a problem. You're right, I should get more involved and I will."

I glanced at my watch and saw that it was getting on to midnight. "I hate to break this up but it's getting late."

She then looked at her watch and said. "My word, I don't believe it. I need to get home myself I have an early morning class. They say when time rushes bye, that it's a good sign. I truly enjoyed getting together with you Greg."

"I feel the same way. Let me pay the bill and we'll be on our way."

I surprised myself that evening. I had no trouble talking to her since she made me feel relaxed and at ease. And by the end of the night, I felt like I had known her all my life.

It was well after midnight by the time I drove her home. I escorted her to the door while holding her hand, which she allowed me to do. Just like Frank told me, and then decided to give her a quick kiss since she let me hold her hand. If she wouldn't allow me to hold her hand, I wouldn't have kissed her. But before I kissed her, I still had to ask for permission. Remember this was my very first involvement with a woman or girl. "Do you mind if I kiss you?"

She laughed and jokingly said "No."

I hung my head down like a little kid who was denied a bag of candy and nervously said. "I didn't think so."

She laughed, "Greg, I'm only kidding. I'd like that very much." Like I said, Joan had a great sense of humor.

After kissing her for the first time, I was still holding her hands. She looked deeply into my eyes and with a coyest smirk on her face said, "I bet you can do better than that."

The second time, I gave her a deep long kiss. As her breasts pressed against my body, it was like fourth of July fireworks. My heart was racing so hard, I thought it was going to pop out of my chest.

When I had finished, she said, "Now that's what I call a kiss. See you in school tomorrow Greg."

"See you then Joan."

As she was about to close the door, she turned to me and said. "And don't forget, we have a join presentation to make on Thursday."

"So, you're going to hold me to it?"

With a smile on her face she said, "You bet I am."

When I drove home, I was on cloud nine, waking on air, like I had just been to the moon. I had never experienced anything like it before in my life. My first date with a girl and what a girl.

When I walked through the door, Frank was in the living room, watching the news.

When he saw me with a shit eating grin on my face

he said, "I don't have to ask you how things went, I can see they went very well by the look on your face."

I was so excited I could hardly talk. "It did, thanks to all your good advice."

"Glad I could help. Sounds like it was love at first sight?"

"It is Frank. I never met anyone like her."

Frank laughed. "How could you know? You never had a date before."

I and Joan continued to date over the next few weeks.

My time was up with Mary and I left her office feeling real good about my memories of my wife Joan.

When I met with Mary the next week, Larry was still drinking heavily He seemed to be in a continuous stupor. It was hard to have a conversation with him. Nick? Well Nick was Nick. Getting into one fight after another.

Nothing had changed with my two roommates. I couldn't take it anymore. Enough was enough, so I decided to move out. I couldn't stand being around them anymore.

31

THE PRESENTATION

Days before my presentation, I rehearsed and rehearsed. I wanted to get it right so that I could impress my new-found love. I couldn't begin to tell you how nervous I felt, since I had never spoken to a group the size of my class or any group. I continued to meet with the writing group which I enjoyed. The group helped me to build confidence in relating to people.

Before the presentation, I met with Joan at the college coffee shop before our class.

She began the conversation with, "Well, you all set to do it?"

I shook my head. "I don't know Joan; my nerves are frayed. I've been working very hard on it." I sighed. "I guess I'm as ready as I'll ever be."

Joan put her arm around my shoulders and said. "Come on Greg, you're a bright guy. When you look at the class focus on something at the back of the room, that will help you block out the faces of our classmates. I'll be going on first and then I'll turn it over to you. Just tell them the results of our research. Okay?"

"Fine but what If they ask me questions?"

"We can both take them. Remember, this is a joint presentation."

"I just hope I don't mess it up and spoil your grade?"

"Greg, believe me, you won't. Just try and relax. Take a deep breath.

We have to get going. It's almost class time."

Mary then said. "It seemed like Joan had a lot of faith in you, more then you had in yourself."

"You have that right. She always had faith in me. Joan was my rock. There were so many things that I never would have gotten through, if it were not for her. With one exception."

"And what was the exception?"

"Not now. Not ready to talk about that right now."

"Okay Greg. Why don't you finish your story? What a happened next?"

"Well, Joan presented first and then it was my turn. It took me awhile for me to get my voice and speak. My hands were trembling. I could hardly hold the papers. The room was dead silence. The professor said to me

"Greg, continue please."

I cleared my throat and finally gained my composure. I did as Joan told me and focused my attention on a picture at the back of the room. I never saw one of my classmates faces.

There were only a few questions asked by my classmates and I had no trouble answering them since I knew the material so well.

"Professor Forman, I still remember his name, turned to us and said "Well done. You folks did a good job. Who wants to do the next presentation before the class ends?"

Mary then said, "So, what did you get as a grade?"

"Believe it or not we got an A for the project."

As I was leaving the classroom and walking to my car, Joan said, "We did it partner. We did it." She kissed me right in the hallway as students were passing by us. I blushed but it felt Soooo good.

I then looked at Joan and said. "How about celebrating our success by going out for dinner next week?"

She smiled. "I thought you'd never ask."

When I got home, Mrs. O'Shea, mom, was so proud of me getting an A on the project, that she baked one of my favorite pies, a blueberry pie. And Frank gave me $20.00 dollars. That night, instead of eating at home, Frank took me and mom, to a wonderful Italian restaurant, which was something we seldom did. Usually Mrs. O'Shea would object to going out to eat but that night she gladly relinquished her culinary duties.

At this point in my life, at the tender age of 18, I was on top of the world. My life had totally turned around. I couldn't believe it. I was in college, doing well in all my classes, I met my dream girl, had adopted a wonderful mother, Mrs. O'Shea and the construction business was booming.

32

CHRISTMAS AT THE SHELTER

A week before Christmas, the shelter was going to have a party, which would be organized by the volunteers and staff. It would be taking place in the evening at 6:00pm. Gifts would be provided for all the men from St. Margaret's Church. This was a traditional annual event. The shelter had a ten-foot-high Christmas tree and the dining room hall was decorated with streamers, Christmas wreaths and other decorations. The tables were covered with white linen table cloths and napkins rather than the usual paper goods. This represented my first Christmas at the shelter. Holiday music filled the hall and a children's choir was to perform following the meal.

The night of the party, it was about 5:00 pm that evening and Nick and Larry were sacked out on the floor. I went over and shook them up.

Nick angrily responded to my shaking him out of his reverie.

"Professor what the hell are you doing? Can't you see I'm trying to sleep?"

With the excitement of the holiday season, I said. "Nick, tonight's the Christmas party down at the shelter. Let's go."

I could hear the annoyance in his voice as he said. "Party? I don't want to go to any party. Christmas means nothing to me."

"But you can at least enjoy the food. I heard from some of the men at the shelter, that they go all out. Great food and even gifts."

"Christmas? What a joke. The last time I spent Christmas was with my mom before she died. Christmas. Jesus never did anything for me except to give me a hard life. Why should I go celebrate his birthday?"

His bitterness and anger came flowing out of his mouth like waters cascading over Niagara Falls.

I then went over to shake Larry. "Come on Larry. Come with me to the party. It will do you good."

Larry was still feeling the effects of the booze and with slurred speech said. "No Professor, I'll pass."

"Come on Larry. Get up. You could use a good meal."

Nick became angry with my trying to urge Larry to come to the shelter. He turned to me and said. "Leave him alone Professor. Can't you see he don't want to go."

I responded to him with my own anger. "Shit. I've had it with you guys. I think I'm going to find myself some new roommates. You guys are a bunch of losers."

Sarcastically Nick replied. "But we're happy losers. Since you're been getting help from that fancy broad, you've gotten all high and mighty with us."

I didn't like his remarks about Mary. "Watch your mouth Nick. Mary is a good person. She's helped me a lot and she could help you, if you'd let her."

With a laugh he replied. "You sure you're not getting something else from her other than therapy?"

Following that remark, I completely lost my cool. I could no longer contain my anger. "You son of a bitch. Don't you talk to her like that." I hit him.

Nick continued to laugh and taunt me. "Now I know you're getting a little pussy." and laughed uncontrollable.

33

DISASTER

After I left the factory, to go to the Christmas party, I definitely knew I had to find a new place to hang. Especially after the way Nick talked about Mary.

As I walked to the shelter, a light snow began to gently fall over my shoulders and baseball cap. It felt good. It made me think of past Christmases, I use to spend with my brother and Mrs. O" Shea, my mom.

Mrs. O'Shea was a very special person and extremely religious. She would always make sure that Frank and I attended church. And on Christmas Eve we would go to the Midnight mass.

Suddenly, my thoughts shifted from Frank and Mrs. O'Shea to my own family on Christmas morning. I began to remember the joy of seeing my kids open their presents. The smell of a real pine tree. The scones that Joan would make special for the holiday. These images were so clear and real, I felt that I could reach out and touch them. But when I went to reach out for them, I only felt the wet cold air on a snowy night.

I continued to walk towards the shelter. As I

approached the building, the bright and colorful Christmas lights lit up both the outside and inside of the building. When I walked through the doors, I was greeted with the sounds of music and people laughing and singing. The place was alive and filled with joy which was a stark contrast from the men I had left at the factory.

I said hello to some of the guys I had met at dinner or slept next to on the bunks and then I saw Mary, who was dressed in a colorful dress of Christmas green with a corsage of pine and flowers that adorned her dress.

When she saw me, Mary immediately come over to give me a holiday greeting. "Merry Christmas Gregory. So glad you came.".

"Thank you. It feels good to be here."

She looked around the shelter before saying. "Where's the rest of your friends? I surely thought they would come, if only for the food and music."

"That's a long story, for another time. But right now, I want to enjoy the evening. This place looks great. It really makes me feel like Christmas."

"Can I get you some eggnog?"

"No eggnog for me. I haven't had a drink for the last month and I want to keep it that way."

Mary laughed. "Gregory, you know we wouldn't serve alcohol at this place. This eggnog is alcohol free."

I laughed and said. "In that case, I'd love some."

She returned my laugher. When she came back with my drink I said. "Merry Christmas Mary." And she responded in kind.

"I have to tell you Mary, it feels really good to be celebrating Christmas. It was always one of my most favorite holidays. As I stand here, sipping eggnog, things almost feel normal."

Mary Replied. "That's a good sign Greg, to feel normal. So, what's going on with you?"

"I'm going to move out of the factory."

I could see the look of disbelief on her face. "Really? Wow. It really is surprising. I thought you were very tight with Nick and Larry."

"Past tense. I was but I don't want to be with those guys any more. They're Losers. I just can't be around them. They takes me down."

"I thought you three were inseparable."

"We were but things change."

"That's too bad but I think it's a wise move. Maybe I can get you some work and your own apartment."

"Maybe. Never thought of that but it might be a good idea. But not right now"

The joy and happiness of the party was soon interrupted when a staff person came running to Mary. "Mary, I need to talk to you. There's been a problem, a serious problem otherwise I wouldn't be here."

"A problem? What kind of a problem? Excuse me Gregory."

"Something at the factory. You know the place where many of the guys hang out."

At the word factory, my ears perked up. "A problem at the factory. I want to hear what he has to say Mary."

Reluctantly she allowed me to listen in knowing that my friend lived at the factory. Mary then said. "Let's take this to my office."

I couldn't imagine what it was. I wondered if it involved Nick or Larry. How serious was it?

We went into Mary's office where the staff person

John Stalford said. "One of the young guys at the factory tried to take his own life. I don't know if he's going to make it. He was rushed to the hospital just a few minutes ago. He was one of the men who use to come to the shelter."

34

SUICIDE

My heart started race uncontrollable, my hand became moist with sweat. I wondered. *Could it be Larry or Nick?* I reluctantly asked the question. "Do you know who it is?"

"I'm not sure. Some guy by the name of Rick or Nick brought him in."

My face turned white when I heard him mention Nick's name.

I turned to Mary and said. "Mary, you have to drive me to the hospital. I think it is Larry. Larry doesn't have any friends except Nick. It has to be Larry."

"Okay. Let's go with my car."

Mary drove to the hospital as my heart raced with anticipation. If Larry dies, I will never forgive myself. I shouldn't have a said I was leaving. As we approached the main entrance, thoughts of guilt again danced through my head. I kept thinking that I should have seen it coming. Why didn't I do something about it? But then my thoughts were countered with the reality that I couldn't have done anything about it. No matter what I said, he still would have attempted suicide. It just seemed like my life has been consumed with one feeling, guilt. Mary immediately tried to console me as we entered the doors to the hospitals. She saw that my anxiety was getting out of control.

"Gregory, take it easy. He was alive when they took him to the hospital. That's a good thing. Maybe this will motivate him to get help. It just might be a good thing."

"I guess you're right. I don't know anything anymore.

You know Mary, I just can't stop thinking about Larry. Poor Larry. Born from some guy his mother got money for to have sex with. A mother who continually rejected him. They say, only a mother can love her child. Well, that wasn't the case with Larry or my own mother. Larry had lost all hope because of the final rejection by his mother. All hope. I can't leave him now. I can't leave the factory. I feel like I have some crazy obligation or responsibility to both him and Nick."

We took the elevator up to the third floor which was the medical Psychiatric unit. The door was locked so I knocked on the door to get the attention of the aide. He eventually came to greet us. He was a six-foot, stocky male aide, who was dressed in whites with an unwelcoming and annoyed look in his face. He abruptly said, "What do you want?"

I quickly answered, "I'm here to see my friend Larry."

"Sorry. That's not possible. Only official personnel and family are allowed. Besides, he's very sick, in tough shape."

Mary then pulled out her Shelter identification card and flashed it in his face. With authority she replied,

"I'm with the homeless shelter and I'm here to see my client." She lied a little, since Larry was never her client. She hardly knew him except through me.

After seeing Mary's credentials, the aide shook his head in disgust and reluctantly let us in, locking the door behind us.

We were escorted through the hallway with its white antiseptic walls to the nurse's desk. The nurse was busily writing in a patient's chart. I anxiously asked, "How's my friend Larry doing? Is he going to be okay?"

She then asked. "Who are you? Are you family?"

I said "no but..." before I could finish the sentence she said. "I can't tell you anything unless your family."

Mary again stepped in with her credentials in hand saying. "I'm here on official business. This man is a client of mine at the shelter. I want to know what happened and the status of his condition."

The nurse paused for a few seconds before saying. "That's different. Your man tried to cut his wrists with a piece of broken glass. Lucky for him, the guy that was with him, tore off his shirt and wrapped it around his wrist to stop the bleeding and then had someone call an ambulance. If he hadn't act so quickly, he would have died. His condition is stable but he lost a lot of blood but he'll recover. You can go in to see him but we had given him a sedative. He's in no condition to talk. We also had to restrain him to the bed."

Mary turned to me and said, "You heard what the nurse said, do you still want to see him?"

"Yes, yes, I have to. I need to see him with my own eyes."

She told us the room number and we quickly walked to his room. Larry was in a single bed with no other patients. When we walked into his room, he was resting peacefully, in his hospital clothing and was covered with a sheet and blanket. I immediately saw the bandages around his wrist where he had cut himself.

I gingerly approached him and quietly whispered. "Larry. It's the professor."

No reply.

I tried again but he still didn't respond to my voice. He was unconscious because of the medication. Like the nurse said, he was in no condition to talk.

Mary seeing my distress, put her hands on my shoulder and said, "Let's go Gregory, there's no sense trying to talk to him. Can't you see that? You saw him. Now let's go."

I shook my head and said, "I know. I just want to stay a few more minutes by myself if you don't mind?"

"Okay I'll be waiting in the hallway."

I again began to speak, "Larry. I'm sorry for what happened. When you get better, we can get you some help. I'll stay with you and visit again. I love you. I can more than understand what it's like when a mother rejects her child. You know it happened to me but you can't give up. You need to pick up the pieces and go on. You hear me? I'm not going to abandon you like your mother did. I promise, I'll always be with you, and be your friend.

I then gently stroked his arm. "Take care buddy. See you again. Nick and I will be rooting for you. Praying for your recovery." I than left.

By the time we reached the shelter, the Christmas party was over.

I went to bed that evening feeling physically and emotionally drained. I made a promise to Larry to stick with him and I had every intention to keep that promise.

My sleep that night was a restless one. I had terrible dreams of my friend's funeral. In my dream, Larry died and they were having the funeral at the factory. People kept pointing to me, saying that it was all my fault. He was my friend and I deserted him. I should have done something to save his life but I didn't.

35

VISITING LARRY

The next few days, I was in the factory getting ready to go to the hospital, when I turned to Nick and apologized to him for getting so angry at both him and Larry and my threatening to leave the factory. I deeply expressed my appreciation for his saving Larry's life.

I said. "You know, when I was yelling at you and Larry, I just wanted to see you guys get better. I was concerned about you."

Nick shook his head. His tone was very serious. "I know you were concerned about us and I shouldn't have been such a wise ass with my comments. I shouldn't have made those comments about your therapist. You know me Professor, I can be very flip with my comments. I'm sorry for what I said."

I went over to him and said." Let's put it all behind us and think about Larry. I'm going to see him now and I hope you'll come along with me."

He shook his head, saying. "I don't know Professor. You know me and hospitals don't mix very well."

I pleaded with him to come with me. "But just a

brief visit, to say hello. I went the other day and he was out cold. I figure now it's been a few days. He should be able to talk to us."

"Tell you what Professor, I'll go for five minutes and then leave. That's it."

"Thanks Nick. I know he'll want to thank you for what you did. He certainly will appreciate the visit."

Christmas had passed along with the snow, but the weather remained cold and crisp. As we went to the bus stop, the cold air rushed over our faces, turning them red. Our lips were turning blue. Of course, all we were wearing, was some torn old jackets and wool watch caps, that didn't provide much protection against the inclement weather.

We got off the bus and approached the hospital entrance. I looked at Nick, whose anxiety was increasing with each step he took towards the direction of the hospital.

I turned to him and said. "It'll be okay pal. We're almost there. Just five minutes and then you can leave."

When we approached the nurse' desk, we asked to see our friend.

There was no problem with us visiting him. She directed us to another floor, the psychiatric ward, since Larry had sufficiently recovered from his wound. When we reached the door to the unit, the attendant freely let us inside. We told the attendant that we were here to see Larry.

"Good. Why don't you follow me to his room?"

"Thank you."

As we went through the common area, Nick stayed close to me. He had experienced a psychiatric ward before and it still bothered him even thou he wasn't the patient. Some of the men were obviously hallucinating, responding to imaginary voices. Others were nervously pacing the floor. Still other patients, sat in their chairs staring into space. It looked like something out of a horror movie.

I turned to Nick and reassured him, "you're doing good Nick."

When we came to his room, Larry was sitting on a chair with his eyes closed as if he was meditating.

I went over to him and gently shook his shoulder, saying, "Larry, it's us, the professor and Nick."

He slowly raised his head up. When he saw the two of us, a smile embraced his face. He couldn't believe what he was seeing.

He kept repeating the words in disbelief. "Professor? Nick? What are you guys doing here?"

"We came to see you. We're family. Remember?"

He looked confused. "Professor, I thought you didn't want to have anything to do with us."

"That's changed Larry. I made a mistake. I'm here to ask you to forgive me. What can I say?"

He let out a little chuckle before replying, "Of course, I do. You're forgiven."

"Larry, do you know what happened to you?"

"Not everything but some. I guess I tried to cut myself, kill myself. You know professor, I just had it with life. But I screwed up. Imagine that, I can't do anything right, not even kill myself. I remember that you were with me Nick. You saved my life, didn't you? You wrapped something around my wrist and then I passed out."

"That's right. Nick saved your life. He stopped the bleeding and got an ambulance to take you to the hospital."

Larry looked puzzled. "Nick. You did that for me?"

"Sure did buddy. I didn't want to lose one of my only friends. All we have is each other."

A look of confusion drifted over Larry's face. "But why didn't you just let me die? I'm no good to anyone. I'm just a piece of shit."

I put my arms around him and said. "Larry, you mean something to us. You're important to us. Now that you're here at the hospital, you can get the help you need, so you can begin to have the life you deserve."

For the very first time I saw a glimmer of hope in Larry's face. He smiled. "Do you really think they can help me?"

"I know they can."

I looked over at Nick who was getting antsy. I knew he was jumping out of his skin. He could no longer remain at the hospital, even for Larry.

"Nick, you can leave now if you want?"

He looked at Larry and said. "Okay buddy. I got to go. You know me and hospitals don't mix. Get better soon pal."

Nick gave him a hug and Larry responded by saying. "Thanks Nick. I owe you."

As he was walking out the door, Nick replied "You sure as hell do." He laughed and left.

Larry then turned his attention towards me. "You staying Professor?"

"Sure. I don't have anywhere to go."

"But don't you have an appointment with Mary?"

"I do but that's not until 4:00. I have plenty of time. I again want to apologize for treating you like I did."

"I told you. No need to apologize. I deserved it."

Forcefully I replied, "No, you didn't. You're a good guy. A wonderful person. Your mother had no right to treat you like she did. She's a sick woman Larry. It was her illness that was speaking."

Larry shook his head. "I don't know Professor. I just don't know."

"Well I do know. Stay here, get dried out and see a therapist. You might see things differently after you talk to a counselor. Now is the time to act. Will you do that Larry? Not for me but for yourself."

Larry hesitated for a moment. Before saying, "I guess I can give it a try."

"Great. That's what I wanted to hear. I need to move on buddy but you can be sure, I'll be back. Love you pal."

My comment of love, caused tears to roll down his cheek.

Larry was touched by my remarks. I don't think that anyone ever told this young man that they loved him. So sad. Feeling unloved. Unwanted.

He just couldn't believe what I told him. "You love me?"

"I sure do and I'll be right by your side until you get back on your feet. Until I see a new young man with hopes and dreams."

"Thanks Professor. Thanks. That means a lot to me."

I left the hospital felling relieved that he survived his suicidal attempt and that he now has a chance of getting better. The visit also got me thinking about my own future. *Will I be able to return to a normal and fulfilling life? Will I ever be able to be reunited with my family, my daughter, brother and the only real mother I ever had, Mrs. O'Shea.* These questions and doubts about my own recovery began to swirl around in my head like a storm. I didn't know the answers. I didn't know what would become of me.

36

BACK TO THERAPY

After leaving the hospital, I returned to the shelter, to resume my therapy with Mary. When I walked through the door and looked around at all the old men sitting at the tables in their ragged clothing with the smell of urine and feces, I wondered if that would be my final fate. To be sure, I have made progress but will it continue? I had been able to completely stop drinking, which is a good start. My nightmares have pretty much subsided. I guess these two accomplishments is some kind of evidence that I'm on the right path.

When I reached her office, the door was closed so I gently knocked on it. I was immediately greeted by her wonderfully comforting and calming voice. "Hi Gregory, I'll be finishing up in a few minutes."

I quietly took a seat in the hallway, waiting for Mary to finish with her client. She apparently was running overtime. But that was Mary. Her clients meant everything to her. Her clients came first.

The door finally opened and a man in his seventies

with uncombed gray hair walked out with the help of a cane. Mary assisted him, until he was able to navigate on his own. He graciously thanked her for her time.

"Okay Gregory, why don't you come on in. Sorry for being late but the gentleman needed a little bit more of my time."

"Not a problem. I don't really care how long I have to wait, as long as I can see you."

Mary laughed. "You are such a sweet man. So, tell me how are you doing? Did you see your friend Larry today?"

"Yes, I did. Nick came with me but he didn't stay very long. You know Nick. He gets very anxious around hospitals."

"How was the visit?"

"It really went very well. Larry was surprised to see the both of us. They'll be giving him some therapy to deal with his drinking and emotional problems."

"I'm so happy to hear that. What about you? Would you like to begin where you left off?"

"Yes. That'll be good. We went for pizza and the movies this one Saturday night. It became our usual routine. Things were going strong with the two of us. Our relationship really took off. We seldom had an argument except for this evening, when Joan completely lost her cool. "Okay Greg, we've been going together for eight months and I've yet to meet your family. You keep putting it off. Always telling me, this is not a good time, or that is not a good time. When is a good time? Why won't you let me meet them?"

"I'm sorry Joan. I didn't mean to get you so upset but..."

Joan interrupted before I could finish the sentence

and said "But nothing. What are they, mass murders, bank robbers, people from out of space? Give me one, just one good reason and I'll stop bugging you. Just one."

I tried to calm her down. I hated, when she became upset. "Joan, please settle down." I paused for a moment thinking about what to say. "Joan, my family isn't like your family. They're different."

"What do you mean different? Different in what way? What's with the different."

"Well, for one thing, it's only myself, my brother, and the housekeeper, who has become part of our family."

The expression on Joan's face changed from impatience and anger to sadness. "What happened to your mom?"

Her use of the term mom, caused me to become angry. "You mean the bitch?" Joan was taken aback by my choice of words. I almost never swore when I was around her. "Dad is separated from her. She wasn't a mother and not much of a wife. She was a business woman who was more interested in her career then her family. Following the divorce, it was only my brother Frank and my dad. The three of us got along really well. We were all relieved that my mom was out of the picture. And then life threw us another curve."

"What happened Greg?"

My eyes filled up with tears. The words seemed to get stuck in my throat. The pain that came with the loss of my dad never fully left me. "My dad suddenly died from an accident on the job. We were in shock. It was at that point in my life that I gave up on religion, God and going to church. I felt that God had deserted us. I didn't understand why this was happening to us. Frank was left with the responsibility of running the construction business on his own. I knew nothing about it."

"I'm so sorry to hear that Greg. That must have been awful, to lose your dad especially after what had happened with your mother."

"It took us a long time to get over his loss. He meant everything to us.

You can't believe what a great guy he was. A real special father. It still bothers me to talk about it."

Joan moved from the other side of the booth and sat next to me. She bought her arms around me and softly kissed me.

"I never knew that about you. You never seem to talk about your family and your past life. I am so sorry. I just didn't know."

"Well, I don't like to talk about it. Anyways, after my father's death, my brother and I struggled to keep up the house between the dinners and housecleaning. The place was a complete mess. It looked like a tornado hit it. So, we hired a housekeeper, who was more than a housekeeper. She became a real mom to us. Caring and looking after us."

Joan grew very quiet as I told my story.

"Maybe I was ashamed to tell you about my messed-up family. Maybe you wouldn't like them. You know, I don't have a family like yours with a loving mother and father and siblings."

"Gregory, I love you. And I know I'll love your family. Families are like ice cream, they come in different flavors but they're all families. So, what do you think? When do I meet them?"

I sighed and said, "I know they want to meet you. They have been on my back about it. How about this

Sunday for dinner? I know that Mrs. O'Shea or mom as we call her, always makes enough food. She's a great cook."

Joan kissed me again saying, "I'm looking forward to it.

37

NEED TO SHARE

By the time I got home that Saturday night everyone was in bed. I had become so excited and anxious about Joan coming to dinner tomorrow that I had to tell someone, so I went into Frank's bedroom and woke him up.

Frank was in a deep sleep, I had to shake him vigorously in order to wake him up. "Frank? Frank? Wake Up?"

He was still groggy and his eyes were closed. "What? What? What's wrong?"

"Nothing's wrong but I need to talk to you."

`He then sat up in his bed, confused and said. "Greg what the hell is wrong with you? It's the middle of the night."

"No, it isn't. Only midnight."

"That is the middle of the night for me. So, happening?"

"My girlfriend Joan is coming over the house for dinner tomorrow. I invited her. She wants to meet you and mom."

"You woke me up for that? Great, now, let me go back to sleep."

I continued to talk to him. "Frank. Frank this is special. You need to be on your best behavior. No bad jokes. No wise remarks."

"Alright. Alright. I'll be on my best behavior. Now can I get back to sleep. Before you know it, we'll be going to church. You know mom likes to go to the 9:00 o'clock mass on Sunday."

"Sorry to wake you. I just had to tell someone. Thanks for listening."

Frank tried to return to his treasured sleep. "Sure. Whatever you say."

"Thanks again Frank. I'm counting on you to make a good impression."

Now my brother was starting to get angry with me. "Gregory. I said fine. Let me get back to sleep, please. This is my only day to rest."

"Sorry. Okay Go back to sleep. Thanks."

38

GETTING READY TO MEET JOAN

The next Morning, I got up early. I was so excited about Joan coming to the house, that I couldn't sleep. I even got up before mom, and made the coffee.

When mom came downstairs dressed in her blue housecoat with curlers in her hair it was about 7:00am. When she saw me in the kitchen, she was shocked? "What in all of heaven are you doing up at this hour of the day Mr. Gregory?" She called me Mr. Gregory when she was angry or confused about my behavior.

"Mom, I hope you don't mind but I invited my girl-friend over for dinner today. I was hoping that you could make her something special. You know, this is important to me. She's been wanting to meet our family for a long time."

"Well she doesn't have to do any more waiting. I've been hoping to meet her for months. It's about time you brought her around. I'm so happy for you Gregory."

"Thanks mom. So, can you make a special meal for her?"

"Of course. All my meals are special."

"I know they are but I mean something real special."

I just happen to have a pot roast in the freezer. I can take it out and serve it with mashed potatoes, string beans and lemon meringue pie for dessert. Will that do it Master Gregory?"

I ran over and hugged and kissed her. "You're the best mom. The very best."

"Now, would you mind Mr. Gregory, if I get dressed so we can go to church. It is Sunday after all. You know?"

"I'm sorry. Sure. Sure."

"You don't have to bother with breakfast mom, we can just have cereal today."

"That won't do. When you brother comes down-stairs, he'll want a real breakfast. Afterall, you know he works long days and very hard. Now stop you're worrying and get ready for church. Everything will be okay."

"I guess you're right."

"You can help, by getting the meat out of the freezer so it will begin to defrost."

"What time will we be eating?"

Let's say 1:00 instead of noon. I will need a little more time to get things ready."

I went over and gave her another kiss, saying "Thanks again mom."

"Never mind all the kisses, get going."

We had breakfast that morning and went to church. Mom began to put the meal together. I helped her peel the potatoes and prepared the string beans.

When it was 12:30am, I left to pick up Joan at her home. When I came to her door and rang the bell, Joan greeted me with a kiss and said. "I'm ready. Let's go."

While we were driving, to my house I said. "I hope you love pot roast and mashed potatoes?".

"Actually, I love pot roast, especially with mashed potatoes. My mom makes it sometimes."

My nerves had taken over my mouth. I started talking non-stop. Joan clearly saw my anxiety and said. "Stop it Gregory. I'm sure I'll like anything your mom prepares. And I'll love your family. Just relax. Please?"

"Okay. I guess I'm just a little up tight."

"Just a little? That's an understatement."

When we finally arrived at my house, we walked up the walkway and I opened the door to let her in.

39

THE VISIT

As we entered the house we were cordially greeted by mom, Mrs. O'Shea and my brother.

Frank Approached her and politely said, "let me take your coat."

"Thank you."

He continued to speak. "I'm so happy to finally get to meet you. You're all Frank talks about. For a while I thought you were a figment of his imagination. A fantasy."

She laughed and I looked at Frank and said. "Frank. Remember your promise."

"Okay. I'll be on my best behavior." His remarks caused Joan to again burst into laughter again.

I ushered Joan into the living room. Mom stood there before moving or saying a word, waiting to be formally introduced to Joan by me. Realizing that I had failed to introduce her I said. "O Joan, this special lady is our mom as we call her. She's our adopted mother. She was known as Mrs. O'Shea before she came to help us out."

Joan said "Mrs. O" Shea, I am so happy that I finally get to meet you."

"You can call me mom. I'm happy you accepted Gregory's dinner offer. Gregory, she is a beautiful woman. I like her right away."

Joan blushed at mom's compliment. I said mom, "you're embarrassing her."

"Why? She is beautiful. I'm just telling the truth."

We took our seats in the living room. Mom than asked her, "Could I get you something to drink, fruit juice or sodas. What's your preference?"

"A coke if you have it, would be fine."

She then turned to my brother Frank. "Frank, you want your beer?"

"Sounds good to me mom."

I then said. "That sounds good to me mom. I'll have one."

She quickly replied to my request. "And a tonic for you Mr. Gregory."

She soon returned to the living room with the drinks, cheese and crackers and potato chips."

Mom, being the perfect hostess said to Joan, "Have something to eat dear while I get the dinner ready?"

"Why thank you. I will."

Mom then said. "I like this girl Gregory, she has good manners. That tells me a lot about a person."

During the dinner mom really began the Irish inquisition.

"So, Joan, are you Catholic dear?"

Joan was taken aback by the direct question and initially stumbled around for the words. "Yes, I am."

"Well that's a good thing."

Her comments caused Frank to burst into laughter

Mom proceeded with her questioning. Never missing a beat. "And do you go to church regularly?"

I had to intercede because I knew the answer might not please mom., "Mom, give her a break."

But my mother persisted with her question. "I'm just trying to make conversations. So, do you?"

"Not always, When I'm at school my life gets very busy."

"Well you know it's important to go to church."

I had to change the subject before the questioning got completely out of hand. "Mom, did you know that she has is one of five children?"

"No, you never told me that. That's what I call the perfect family. I would have liked children myself but God didn't bless me with such fortune."

The evening continued with mom hammering Joan with question after question about her family and background. Frank told her about our construction business and how my dad built it from scratch, to be very successful.

When the afternoon finally came to an end, it was about 4:30 in the afternoon. I said to mom, "Well, Joan has homework to do for tomorrow so I better get her back home."

Mom and Frank gave her a hug and kissed her on the cheek and we left. I immediately began to apologize to Joan for all of my mom's questions.

Joan laughed. "Not a problem. I love her and your brother Frank sounds like a great guy. They're such good people. Do you feel better now Gregory, that its over? You survived the day."

"I do. As you can see mom is a devote Catholic. She was born in Ireland and came to this country as a child. Religion has always been central to her life."

"I can see that and I respect her, for her convictions. So, Gregory, I'll see you tomorrow at school?"

"You sure will."

I gently hugged her and kissed her goodnight.

She responded by saying. "That was a wonderful time Gregory. I really enjoyed myself. I love your family.

"Thanks. See you tomorrow."

I left her house and drove home feeling a great weight was lifted off my shoulders. That's the way life goes. We sometimes tend to anticipate the worse but the worst doesn't always happen.

40

LARRY MAKES PROGRESS

Before going to the shelter, I decided to drop in and see Larry. Of course, Nick refused to come with me. He was still drinking heavily which continued to concern me along with his fighting. It seemed that that every week he would get into a fight with some of the other men at the factory or on the street. A remark, or the way someone looked at him the wrong way would result in a fight.

I took the elevator up to the fourth floor, the psychiatric unit. Larry was now on an open unit. No more locked doors. I went to the nurse's desk and asked to see Larry since he wasn't in his room.

The nurse said. "He's in group. He should be out shortly. You can take a seat in the common room, over there."

Before I left the nurse's station, I told her I was a good friend of his and wondered how he was doing. She smiled and said, "It's remarkable, the kind of progress he's made in such a short period of time."

I thought to myself, *Larry seems to be doing much*

better than me. Maybe I should sign myself into the wacky ward.

After waiting for 30 minutes, Larry came walking into the room with a grin on his face. I had never seen Larry look so good in all the time I've known him. He had on new clothes, a long sleeve shirt, sweater, dungarees and new sneakers. Quite a difference, from when I last saw him. He also had a haircut and was cleaned shaven.

When he saw me, he became excited and gave me a hug and said. "Professor, it's so good to see you again. Things must be slow. You've been up here a lot."

I smiled back and said. "You have that right. Not much happening at the factory and begging for coins has been slow and cold. Nick stills get drunk and fighting his way through life. You're nice and warm in here but outside it's 32 degrees. We're supposed to get some snow tomorrow. Maybe 3 to 4 inches. Larry, I have to say this place agrees with you. You look and sound like a new man."

"Professor, this is the best thing that ever happened to me. I mean the people here are terrific. There are all kinds of people like me, who want to get better.

"Tell me, what it's like?"

"We have group, five days a week to start with."

"And what do you do in group?"

"We talk about our problems and our struggles. We also talk about going out on our own. Working. Imagine that getting a job. I never had a real job in my whole life. They have a job training center nearby where they teach you a trade or skills. I never thought this would happen to me Professor."

As Larry talked, he was filled with enthusiasm. I said. "Wow. That's great."

He was talking so fast the he could hardly get the words out of his mouth. "And then I see a therapist twice a week, a social worker. You know just like Mary."

"From what you're saying, sounds like this place has been very good for you."

"I can't begin to tell you how much it has helped me. When I talk to my social worker, her name is Helen, I tell her about my shitty life and leaving home and why I tried to commit suicide. She listens. Imagine that? She pays attention to every word I say."

"I know what you mean. Mary does the same thing with me. It's nice to have someone, who gives you their full attention."

"But you know Professor, the one thing I got out of it all?"

"What's that?"

"Hope. Just plain hope for a better life. Something I had never experienced in all my years."

I thought to myself, *hope is something I haven't had for a long time.* "She made me realize that my mother is a sick woman. She didn't mean to treat me like she has. It's her illness. You know?"

I jokingly said. "I know. It doesn't look like you'll be returning to the factory."

"Not a chance. I'm on my way to a greater and better life. Being homeless isn't for me anymore."

"I'm so happy for you Larry. You deserve it, all of it."

Larry continued to talk with unending enthusiasm. "As a matter of fact, my social worker says when I'm ready to get a job, they're going to send me to a group home to live. And if I do well at the home, they'll find me my own place." His excitement would continue to rise as he talked about his future. "My own place. Than you and Nick will be able to visit with me. I can cook a real meal for you guys and I....."

"Slow down partner. Slow down. You're like a run-away freight train."

"I'm sorry Professor. I'm just so happy."

An hour had passed before I said to him. "Larry, I have to go. I have an appointment with Mary. I almost forget the time."

"I know. It's been great talking to you Professor. And how is it going with you and Mary?"

"Not bad. Things are moving slowly but they're moving. Like you, I always feel better after talking to her."

"Don't worry Professor, you'll get there. I know you will"

"I hope so. Like I said, things are not moving as fast as with you."

Larry gave me a hug and walked me to the door.

"Keep the faith Professor. Keep the faith."

"See you Larry. I'll be back in a few days."

"Look forward to it."

After leaving the hospital I felt happy for Larry but was saddened by the fact that my recovery wasn't moving as fast as his. Maybe hospitalization is the key. But I couldn't do that.

When I heard him talk about getting a job and his own place it didn't make me feel very good. I mean, I felt good for Larry but not for me. I thought to myself *that should be me. Why can't I get out of this hellhole, the factory?* Why? It bothered me as I walked all the way back to the shelter to meet with Mary. I kept thinking about the why in my life.

41

THE ENGAGEMENT

After leaving Larry I went straight to the shelter to keep my appointment with Mary. As I walked along the street, the wind and cold nipped at my face. The winter seemed to be singing a song of hopelessness just for me. I should be happy for Larry and I shouldn't be complaining about myself. It's almost as if I felt jealous over what Larry has accomplished.

When I arrived at the shelter and entered her office, Mary immediately picked up on my distress. Like I said, she was always able to read my feeling before I even uttered a word. I took a seat in front of her desk.

"Gregory, you look troubled. What is it?"

"No big deal. Just feeling sorry for myself. I went to the hospital to see Larry today. He's doing great. And he's so happy. I mean really happy about what he's accomplished."

"I don't understand. Your friend is doing very good and you're despondent?"

"I am but..." I paused

"But what?"

"I don't feel like I'm making as much progress as Larry. Why? Mary Why?"

"Gregory I can appreciate your impatience but you need to realize that we are all different as a people and we react differently to our problems. But I do feel you're making progress. It may seem slow but you are getting there."

"But I should be thinking about getting a job and living on my own. Larry said he's looking forward to getting training and a job. He was all excited about leaving the hospital. You know what I'm trying to tell you?"

"I do Gregory. You'd like to be like your friend and leaving the factory and the shelter."

"Exactly."

"That will come in good time. You have suffered some kind of serious trauma that brought you to the streets, that made you homeless. I don't know what it is yet but we'll get at it. We'll get at it when you're ready. What do you think?

"I guess."

"Do you want to continue where you left off or do you want to talk about what's bothering you some more?"

"No. No. Let me finish my story. I think it will help you better understand who I am and what brought me to the factory."

"Okay. Sounds like a plan."

It was amazing how fast my time in college flew bye. I loved learning and my classes. I loved college. Mary and I were still going strong. I was about to enter my senior year and then I'd be going on for my Masters. We had talked about marriage off and on but now it was time to set a date. It was August. I felt it was time for me to ask Joan to become my wife. I was hoping that she would accept my proposal.

I wanted to ask her in the most creative way possible. To be extra special and romantic therefore I proposed to her at a Red Sox's game."

Mary laughed. "At a baseball game? Didn't sound very romantic?"

"I know it sounds strange but you need to understand, we were both big Red Sox fans. We loved to watch the games when we weren't studying. My brother Frank was able to get us two tickets to a game, right along the third baseline. He got the tickets from one of his customers for the August 18th game, which was on a Saturday. It was perfect. I called Joan up Friday evening and asked if she would be interested in going. She immediately became very excited and jumped at the chance to go to a Red Sox game, especially with such great seats. When I told her where we would be sitting, she practically came through the phone. We had both limited funds so she wasn't expecting to go to game, never mind tickets on the third baseline.

That Saturday morning, I happened to be home for the weekend. I liked to spend the weekend at home with my family. I borrowed my brothers' car and picked her up at the dorm.

She greeted me with one long kiss, which I came to love and expect.

"Greg, this is fantastic. That was the last thing I was expecting to do this Saturday. On the third baseline no less? You must have spent a small fortune for those tickets."

"To be honest with you, Frank got these tickets for

us from one of his customers. I thought it was time to put our books aside and have some fun. We both having been spending's lot of time studying.

"You're certainly right about that. Okay. I'm set. Let's get moving."

We drove to the game in Boston and I found a parking space on Commonwealth Ave. about a mile away from the game.

"Sorry for the long walk but I didn't want to spend my money on a parking lot."

"Not a problem. It's such a nice day for a walk."

And it was.

We reached the park following a long but pleasant walk, and proceeded to take our treasured seats. The sky was blue with not a single cloud. The temperature was a warm 84 degrees. Maybe a little too warm with the sun beating down on us but nevertheless it felt good. Boston was playing the Minnesota Twins. We couldn't wait to see some of our favorite players like Wade Boggs, and our all-time favorite Jim Rice, playing left field. They played the National anthem and we all respectfully stood up.

When we were seated, I went and bought a few pretzels and beers for Joan and myself. Before the game began, a loud booming voice made an announcer saying "I would like to direct your attention to the screen."

I was so excited that I could hardly retain my composure. I appeared on the screen along with Joan. Joan looked at the screen and was very surprised at what she saw. She said. "Gregory, that's us up on the screen. What in the world is going on? Why do they have us on the big screen?"

Within seconds she had the answer to her questions.

I got down on my knee while the cameras were poised at Joan and myself and said, "Joan, will you marry me?"

The crowd went crazy when they heard and saw my proposal. Joan turned to me with the tears streaming down her face. She could hardly get the words out of her mouth. Her hands were trembling with excitement as I held them. "Yes. Yes." She kissed and embraced me. The crowd went wild again and the people that surrounded us gave us their congratulations.

It was a great day even if the Sox lost to Minnesota six to four.

Mary laughed at my proposal story. "Gregory that was so creative and unique. How did you do that?"

"I went to the management and told them what I wanted to do. They thought it was a great idea."

That day was a beautiful start to a marriage that ended in any ugly separation.

42

SPREADING THE NEWS

When I came home Saturday at 8:00pm I couldn't wait to tell my family what happened.

Frank and mom were sitting in the living room watching television.

Frank was the first to speak." Hey Greg. How was the game?"

"Great. But I have some news to tell you."

"News, What news?" asked mom.

"I proposed to Joan at the ballgame."

Mom and Frank were confused by what I said. Frank said. "You proposed to her at the ballpark? Did I hear right?"

I then related to them what I had done.

Frank and mom laughed. Mom said. "Gregory, that was so romantic and unique. I never would have thought you would do anything like that."

Frank joined in. "I mean that was amazing. I assume she said yes?"

Mom then said "Let's go into the kitchen where we can talk. I'll put on a pot of coffee." Mom loved her coffee. "And we can have some apple pie that I made today.

I said, "sound great."

So, when will you be getting married?" asked Frank

"Sometime after we finish school and when we both get a job. We figure in about one to two years."

As mom was setting the table with coffee cups, plates and silverware she said. "Gregory, you should wait until you both have a good nest egg. You don't have enough money."

"Mom. We can't wait. We don't want to wait. We love each other"

Mom just shook her head. "I don't know, you young people are crazy.

I laughed, "crazy in love."

Frank then joined the conversation. "Have you guys talked about where you're going to live?"

Probably in Arlington. I didn't tell you that I'll be doing my student teaching in the East Arlington middle school."

Frank said. "So, you're going to be a real live teacher. He then shook his heads saying "I can't believe it Greg, my little brother a teacher."

Mom said. "You worked hard Gregory. You deserve it. It will be nice to have a professional in the house."

Frank looked at her and jokingly replied, "Wait a minute mom. I'm a professional." He was just trying to get a rise out of her.

She came right back. "You know what I mean Frank. Don't be such a wise guy or you won't get any pie."

She then poured the coffee and cut us a piece of pie.

"You both wants some ice cream with that pie?"

"That sounds great mom. Right Frank?"

"You bet and don't be so stingy with the pie."

She laughed. "You funny man. Am I ever stingy?"

"Just joking mom."

She served us the pie with a large scoops of ice cream and then said., "You know Gregory, I like this Joan. She a nice woman and comes from a nice family. Maybe sometimes, since you going to marry her, it would be nice to meet her family."

"That's a great idea."

"Why don't you invite them to the house and I'll make a dinner for them?"

"Sounds like a plan mom."

We then took to the business of devouring her pie which was covered with ice cream.

I was happy that they were pleased with my getting married, that they loved Joan almost as much as I.

Life was looking better with each passing day.

43

THE TEACHER

September brought about the beginning of our last year and then on to my master's degree. I was very excited about doing my student teaching. I was never one for speaking in front of a group, never mind a group of middle school children. I can't lie. I had some reservation on how I would do.

When I saw Joan at school, she approached me.

"So, Gregory, the day is finally here, we get a chance to do some student teaching."

I nonchalantly replied, "Student teaching."

"Greg, what's the matter with you? This is what you always wanted to do. It's going to be fun."

"I don't know Joan. I loved the classroom stuff and learning how to teach but standing in front of a group of kids? I don't know."

"Gregory, you did well, when we did the join presentation."

"But that was different. All I did is speak but to teach. Wow."

She just shook her head and mocking me said.

"There's Gregory, Mr. Worrywart. You have to stop being that way. Always worrying about everything. You need to have confidence in yourself. I have confidence in you."

"Thanks Joan I appreciate that."

"Well. You know what I think your problem is?"

"What's that?"

She laughed. "You worry too much. But seriously, you obsess about things. Let it go. Just do it."

"Maybe your right. But then, you're always right."

"I have to get to class. When will you start?"

"Next week."

"Good. Now don't think about it anymore. Show those kids who's boss."

"And when do you start?"

"The same. Next week. I'll be facing a group of high school sophomores. Now that's a challenge."

"I know. I couldn't deal with them."

"I think you could, if you tried and just relaxed."

"Thanks Joan."

Mary then said, "And how did you do with your student teaching? Did you survive?"

"Fortunately, I did. I was nervous as a cat on a hot tin roof but the teacher in that class was really nice and supportive of me. I had about 22 students. An even mix of boys and girls. I had prepared a lesson plan which the teacher reviewed and thought it was well done. She introduced me to the class and I began. The students to my surprise, were all very attentive for the most part. When I was done, the teacher said I did a great job.

Following the class, one of the young children came up to me and said they liked me and hoped that I would come to teach at their school. That made my day. It made me think of the days when I was in class and how much I, Loved my teacher. It felt good.

44

FAMILY VISIT

Thanksgiving came, Christmas came, New Year's Eve came and soon they were history. We were now in our last semester. It was March when mom said to me, "I think it's time for Joan's family to comer to dinner."

I said "Okay, I'll call Joan and maybe we can set a date in two weeks, if this works for you."

"Wonderful. I will make a special Irish dinner, Corned beef and cabbage. How does that sound?"

"Anything you make sounds great and don't forget to make your famous apple pie. You'll probably need two of them since her brothers and sisters are coming."

She laughed, "Gregory, Joan is right, you're such a worrywart. You know me, I make more than enough food."

When I saw Joan in school, I invited her and her parents to come for dinner. She happily accepted the invitation after checking with her parents. Our families were going to meet each other for the very first time.

She agreed that the meeting was be a good idea.

A few weeks passed bye and that infamous Sunday was soon upon us. When I saw Joan in school on Friday I said. "This Sunday is it. I hope things work out."

"They will Greg. We are lucky to have two great families. Loving families. I know they'll hit it off."

"I hope you're right."

Joan became angry with me. "O shit Greg, here you go again Mr. Worrywart."

"Okay. Okay. No more talk of it."

"That's better."

"So, Joan, how's the teaching going?"

"Greg. I love it. And what about you?"

"I did like you said and put things out of my mind. Didn't try to think about it and it worked."

"I knew it would. Well, got to get to class. See you later."

"At my house this Sunday."

Mary said. "How did it work out with Joan's family?"

45

MEET THE FAMILY

The day the two families were about to meet, mom, myself and, Frank went to the 7:00 o'clock mass even thou Frank complained about going to church so early, that he needed his sleep. But Frank would never go against mom. She made two apple pies and even bought some ice cream to put on top of them in order to satisfy the hungry appetites of her guests. She had gone to the store to buy a corned beef..

My job was to peel the potatoes and prepare the cabbage. I was the designated houseboy, the one who would usually help mom around the house. Frank was absolved from household chores since he had worked all day in the business, a business that supported our family. I had no problems helping mom knowing that I was also helping my brother. He was the primary support for our family. Frank would have sent me to any college I wanted but I insisted on going to a State college.

I waited with anticipation for Joan's family. It was 12:00 noon when the front door bell rang and her family made their entrance.

Mom was in the kitchen still busy, preparing our feast. I yelled out. "I'll get the door. It's probably them."

When I opened the door, I was greeted by Joan's family. I yelled out, "Mom. Frank, the Kelly's are here."

Frank came to the door and greeted them and invited them into the living room. The weather was still cold so Frank politely took their coats.

I told them that our mom would be in shortly and within five minutes when everyone was seated in the living room, mom joined us with a tray of goodies and a pitcher of lemonade. She placed the food on the table and introduced herself. "I'm happy to meet your family Joan. My name is Mary O'Shea, but the boys call me mom."

A puzzled look came over Joan's families' faces.

Mom saw their confusion over the boys calling her mom and laughed. "I know it sounds odd so. Let me explain. I came to help out the Byrnes a few years ago following the death of their dad. Before long they adopted me as their mom and here I am. After I lost my husband, I didn't know what to do with myself so when I saw the ad in the paper advertising for a house keeper, I applied for the job. I went from housekeeper to mom."

Joan's mother responded. "That is the most remarkable story I have ever heard."

Her dad had vigorously agreed with his wife, "Absolutely extraordinary. I'd like to introduce our family. Should I call you mom or Mrs." O'Shea?"

"Mom will do just fine."

"To begin with my name is Harold but my friends call me Harry. This lovely lady is my wife Rebecca but we call her Becky and these are our children. You already know Joan, Samuel is a senior in high school, our daughter Margaret is also in High school. The youngest of the ladies is Mary jane, who just turned 12 and lastly is Larry, the baby of the family, he's 10 years old.

Larry moaned when being introduced as the baby. "Dad, I'm not a baby."

His objection brought a round of laughter from everyone.

After the introductions, the children each said, "It's a pleasure to meet you, mom."

Mom replied. "You have a beautiful family."

We sat in the living room getting to know each other for the next half hour before the stove alarm went off. Mom got up and said, "I think our dinner is ready, excuse me."

She later returned saying. "Dinner is served in the dining room. Please come in".

We all sat down but before we ate, mom said. "We like to say grace before we eat. Gregory why don't you do the honors."

"Sure, mom I will."

Following grace, Joan's mother said. "That is so nice Don't you think Harry?"

"It is. Maybe we should do the same at home."

Mom then brought out the dinner saying, "I hope you like corned beef and cabbage."

Mr. and Mrs. Kelly lit up upon seeing the dinner."

Mr. Kelly said. "Are you kidding? I wouldn't be much of an Irishmen if I didn't like it."

His comments brought forth more laughter.

We ate dinner before retreating to the living room with full bellies.

Joan's parents asked about the construction business. We also talked about Joan's siblings. And then

Mom asked Joan's parents, "Were your parents from Ireland?"

Harold answered. "My parents weren't but my grandparents were. I assume that with a name like O" Shea and your brogue, you were born in Ireland."

Mom laughed. "Yes. And where are your grandparents from?"

"They came from a very small town called Adare."

Mom's yes lit up. "Adare?"

"Yes. Have you heard of it?"

"I certainly did. We lived in the small village next to it. At times my dad would take me to the Castle. Have your parents or grandparents ever talked about the castle?"

"Why yes, all the time."

And mom continued. "We also loved to play at the ruins of the Franciscan monastery."

And so, the conversation went. The Irish connection solidified the relationship between the families.

The afternoon ended with the two families discussing plans for our future wedding.

Mary then said. "Gregory that sounds like quite a gathering, a good time for two families who never met. Did they continue to develop a relationship?"

"They sure did. They would frequently invite us for a fourth of July picnic or someone's birthday. We all became very good friends. Life was perfect."

"And how was your brother Frank doing? It seems like all he does is work."

"I was in my Junior year of high school when Frank decided to make a major business decision that changed his life."

46

FRANK

It was a weekend in October when Frank came home at about 6:00pm feeling very frustrated. And exhausted. Once in the house, he went straight into the living room after changing his clothes. He would never dare sit in the living room without changing his dirty clothes and risk the ire of mom.

I approached him. "Frank, aren't you going to get ready for dinner?"

"Greg I can't do all of this anymore."

I was puzzled by his remarks. "What do you mean?"

He took a deep breath and then said. "It seems like every weekend when I'm not working, I'm doing the books, ordering materials. Our garage is a mess, filled with all my tools and equipment. It's no good. I need to change things."

"I know Frank, you work your ass off. What can I do to help? Whatever you want. I'll do it."

"No Greg it goes beyond you and beyond me."

"When Mom heard what was going on, she quickly

came into the living room. "Frank, what's happening, you look worn out and beside yourself."

"I am mom. I was just telling Greg that I need to do something about the business. I can't carry the load all by myself."

"I've always thought that but I didn't want to interfere. So, what are you going to do?"

"The first thing I'm going to do is rent some space to store my equipment and also have an office with a business phone and office equipment."

Mom said. "I am so happy that you're finally going to do that Frank. The garage, I can hardly move in it with all your stuff."

"I know and that's just the beginning."

"And there's more?"

"Yes. I've decided to hire someone that can help me with the paper work and phones and all that stuff."

Mom again was very supportive of Frank. "I'd say it's about time Frank. For all these years, I've noticed that all you do is work, work, work."

"That's right mom. I'm getting older and I want some free time for myself. I put an ad in the paper for an assistant. Starting tomorrow I'm going to look for some space to rent."

Monday came and Frank was true to his word. He took the morning off from work and a trail of people paraded themselves in front of him, looking to obtain the job. He was looking for someone, who would be willing to work a full eight hours and, knew a little about accounting and wasn't afraid to manage phone calls.

Eventually he found a woman in her twenties without any family ties. She wasn't married and didn't have a boyfriend. Her name was Maria Scarvoni. She lived in Arlington with a friend in her own apartment. She dated but wasn't currently interested in a long-term relationship. She was an attractive 24-year-old woman who had recently left a job at a small appliance dealer, because she wasn't happy about the owner, who was constantly trying to make a move on her. Not only did my brother interview her but she interviewed him. He liked what he saw. A black-haired beauty with a thin figure. She liked to work out in the gym when she wasn't on the job. Enjoyed all kinds of sports and Jazz was her favorite music.

He hired her on the spot. Maria proved to be a tremendous asset to my brother which freed him up, so that he could have some time for himself. She learned the business very quickly and customers liked dealing with her. Now Frank could make good use of his newly freed time. He would go out with his friends to a football or baseball game or to a lounge in Cambridge to meet women and listen to music.

It happened that about six months after he hired Maria, a customer gave him some tickets to a Red Sox game. Frank wanted to reward Maria for doing such a good job since she would often work beyond the eight hours. Frank wanted to pay her for the extra hours but she would not except the money.

Frank then decided to ask her to the game and she gratefully accepted his invitation for dinner and the baseball game.

Since they had such a good time at the ballgame and they enjoyed each other's company, he continued to date her.

Mary then asked me. "So, what did you think about that?".

"I was more than pleased for Frank. Happy that he finally got time to enjoy himself. And I was especially happy that he found a woman like Maria.

Now let me tell you about my wedding."

47

THE MARRIAGE PLANS

Both Joan and I successfully completed our schooling with a Master's Degree in education. Mom and Frank were so proud of me that they took me out at an expensive restaurant in order to celebrate my graduation. Mom objected to the cost of the dinner but Frank said that I deserved the best. Frank wanted it to be just our family. Joan understood why she wasn't invited and didn't feel offended.

Joan and I also were both fortunate enough to get a job right after graduation. I got a job teaching Social Studies in East Arlington's Middle school and Joan received a job at Belmont High School.

It was now time to begin making plans for our wedding. We had already booked the hotel in Waltham but the more difficult job was at hand, making the wedding list. It was not much of a problem for my family since we only had a few relatives. But Joan had an endless parade of cousins, aunts, uncles, neighbors and friends. Frank offered to defray some of the wedding costs but her dad Harry wouldn't hear of it. This was his first daughter to marry and he wanted to make it a memorable day. Frank wanted to do something for us so he decided to pay for our honeymoon, a trip to Hawaii.

We did have some family but we seldom saw them, especially after my dad died. Like I said before, my dad's parents were living in Texas. I asked Frank about having our grandparents came to the wedding. Dad was never close to them since he left home but we both felt it was the right thing to do. I called them and they were now in their eighties and felt the trip would be too much for them but they did send a monetary gift to us.

Once the list was completed, we had 150 people who would be attending our wedding.

Frank and I both had a few friends that we invited. At Bridgewater, I invited some of the people from my writing group who happily accepted my invitation.

On completing the guest list, we went to the hotel to plan for the food and later we hired a band to play at the wedding. We decided on a small combo, that we had heard, when going to some clubs in Cambridge. We asked them to play music that would appeal to everyone and not just the younger crowd. They showed us a play list and we made our selections.

Joan went with her mother and sisters to choose her wedding dress.

There was only one other piece of business that we needed to do to complete the plans, convince mom to buy a dress for the occasion. Mom was a very frugal lady, who didn't like to spend money on things she considered to be foolish like a new dress. Frank was more than happy to buy a dress for her but she continued to refuse to make such a purchase.

This one day, I became frustrated with mom and said. "Mom, you are going to be the mother of the groom, me. I want you to have a new dress and look like the mother of the groom. I want to be proud of you."

She broke down in tears at the idea that I truly considered here to be my mom. She hugged me and finally agreed to get a new dress. Joan's mother helped her make a dress selection.

Mom was happy that I was getting married but at the same time she would miss me. Her family was slowly slipping away from her. Frank was now spending more time with Maria. They were developing a serious relationship. In time they would marry. It was no surprise when Frank took Maria, to the wedding.

When all the arrangements were finally completed, Joan and I went out for a quiet evening dinner. We were exhausted and about to embark on our life together as man and woman.

48

OUR WEDDING DAY

The day finally arrived. Frank and I were getting ready for my wedding while mom was proudly putting on her new dress. Once my brother and I were dressed we went into the living room to wait for mom. The limo would be arriving to pick us up in 10 minutes.

I turned to Frank and nervously said, "Frank. I can't believe that I'm getting married. I'm really feeling uptight." My hands were trembling as I thought about the idea of walking down the aisle.

Frank laughed and gave me a pat on the back. "Settle down brother. You're going to do just fine."

In my anxiety state I made a stupid remark. "You don't understand. I've never been married before."

At those words Frank went into an hysterical laugh. "Greg do you realize what you said? You've never been married before?"

I couldn't help but join him in the laughter. "I guess I'm more nervous then what I thought. What time to you have Frank? The limo will be here shortly. Mom should have been ready by now."

"We have plenty of time brother. The limo can wait, if she's not ready."

At that very moment, mom came through the doors looking as proud as a peacock. She had even gone to the hairdresser, never min d her newly purchased dress..

I turned to Frank and said, "Look at mom. Mom you look beautiful Just beautiful."

Frank joined in and said. "Now aren't you glad we talked you into getting the dress?"

With a grin on her face she said. "You boys are so wonderful to me."

I replied. "Why shouldn't we be good to you? You're our mom. Come here." The both of us warmly embraced her.

At that moment, the doorbell rang. It was the limo. We drove to the church which was overflowing with people, both invited guests and people who came just to observe the wedding ceremony.

Frank was my best man and Joan had her sister Margaret as her maid of honor.

A silence grew over the church as the organist began to play the wedding march. I looked towards the front of the church and saw my bride to be in a stunning but simple white wedding gown and a veil that covered her face. I stood there mesmerized by her loveliness, as I heard the music.

As I began to describe the wedding to Mary, I started to stutter and repeat myself. I said "As the wedding march was being played." I couldn't finish my sentence. My mind was flooded with thoughts of my horrible, terrifying and recurring nightmare. The vivid and real image of my car crashing thorough the church doors and killing people.

Mary immediately recognized my distress. She said. "Gregory what's the matter?"

I didn't respond. It was as if I was in a trance like I had suddenly been transformed into my nightmare.

She then came around her desk and shook me. "Gregory. Gregory. What's happening?"

I finally awoke from my dream like state. I tried to talk. "The nightmare. The nightmare."

"What about the nightmare?"

My nightmare was the same setting as the church where I got married. It never thought of it. I never...I"

"Calm down Gregory. I'm here. You'll be alright."

"I guess I was experiencing some kind of flashback. But it doesn't make sense. When I got married, I never drove my car though the church doors." I then began to cry. "I'm going crazy. Why would I be having such a dream? Why? Maybe I did kill my family. My bride. In some way?"

Mary put her arm around me in pulled me into her breast. "It's okay Gregory. We'll figure it out. You didn't kill your wife or anyone."

I than begin to scream and yell. "You don't know. I did. I did."

She grabbed my hand and said "Come with me. The doctor will give you a shot to calm you down."

"But Mary?"

Firmly she said. "Please come with me Gregory and then we can talk."

The doctor gave me a shot of something which calmed me down.

Once I gained my composure, I said. "What happened to me Mary?"

"I think your unconscious is trying to tell you

something and it's being expressed in the form of a nightmare. Something is going on in your head and we need to find out what it is."

"Okay Mary. Okay. I think I've had enough for today."

"I think you have. Maybe you should try and get some rest after supper. If you ever need to talk, no matter the time of day, come see me or call me. I'm working late on most nights during the week. Tonight, I'll be here until 9:00."

"Thanks again Mary. I can't make it without you."

"Gregory, someday you will. You'll leave this place and have a normal life again. But we need to get at the heart of what's troubling you."

49

THE HONEYMOON

Frank drove us to the airport, to the sounds and noise of the wedding guests wishing us good luck. Once at the airport, we boarded an airplane to San Francisco and then took a second plane to Hawaii. When we approached the Hawaiian airport, the view of the island was spectacular.

I turned to Joan and kissed her. "Here we are in Hawaii. And we're going to be here for a whole week. Pinch me. I must be dreaming."

Joan laughed and said. "I'll do better than that." She kissed me. "Imagine Greg. No kids, no lesson plans. No troubles for a whole week."

Once we landed, we picked up our luggage and then rented a car. We jumped into the rented car with all our luggage and drove to our hotel, which was located in Maui..

Once we reached the hotel, they placed us in the honeymoon suite, provided us with a bottle of champagne, flowers and a basket of fruit.

I turned to Joan and said. "Can you believe it, we're

in Hawaii and were married." I picked her up, swung her around and kissed her. I than carried her over the threshold.

"I love you Joan. I love you" I shouted."

Joan said, "Gregory calm down. I think the whole island knows that you love me."

"I want them to know. I want them to know that we're going to grow old together. And I will still love you even when your old and gray and your body is all wrinkled. You will always be beautiful to me." I kissed her again.

Joan kissed me back and before you know it, we were in the bed excitedly stripping off our clothes, wasting no time making love. I had never had sex with any other women. Joan was my first and I was her first. The softness of her body next to mine was electrifying. When I kissed her, I felt like I was in paradise. When I entered her with love, the two of us were one and will always be one. I had never experienced such feelings in all my life.

After making love, Joan said to me as we laid in bed. "Wow. That was terrific." And she kissed me again.

I was breathless and said. "Wasn't it?"

She then looked at the clock on the nightstand which read 7:00 o'clock. "Honey, don't you think we better go downstairs for supper."

Half in a daze, I said, "For supper? Who wants to eat? Let's continue what we started. I'm just getting started."

Joan laughed. "Honey. We have all week to make love. I'm really hungry."

"I guess, you're right. Kind of think of it, all that exercise has worked up my appetite."

We got dressed and went downstairs to the dining room for supper. I ordered a drink, a southern comfort Manhattan before our meal and she had a class of red wine. It was our first real meal as a married couple.

We raised our glasses and I said. 'Joan, to us. May our love grow with every passing moment."

She responded "I'll drink to that." and we again kissed. I think we did more kissing that day then all the years of our marriage.

Once the meal came, we talked about what we wanted to do tomorrow. I'd never been so happy in all my years. I wished that the honeymoon would last for an eternity.

Once we finished eating, it was about 8:30pm Joan said, "So what's up for tonight?"

"I booked a nightclub tour. It's neat. They take us to two clubs where we watch a show and have a drink."

"Sounds like fun."

"And that's not all. Tomorrow night we're going to a luau."

"Gregory, you're going to wear me out."

"That happens in the evening my love."

She laughed. It was a very busy honeymoon with plenty of love making in between our daily excursions.

Mary smiled and said. "It sounds like it was a wonderful honeymoon and that you loved and still love Joan."

I couldn't answer for a few minutes. I just went silent. She was right. I had never stopped loving Joan.

I didn't respond to her statement but continued my story, relating to her, what happened after the honeymoon.

Mary interrupted me. "I get the feeling that Joan

and what happened later in your family is something that you're not comfortable talking about."

"Not now. When we returned home, Frank took us to our Waltham apartment. It was a small two-bedroom apartment with a kitchen, small dining area and living room. Small but good enough for the two of us. I again carried her over the threshold as I did in Hawaii.

Joan laughed. "My. My. What a gentleman."

Once inside I said to Joan, "Can you beleive it? This is our home.". I guess we need to buy some groceries so we *can* cook our first meal."

Joan turned to me and put her arms around me. She then gently kissed me. "Our first meal."

Joan's first meal was a disaster but I contributed to the disaster. She was making a ham dinner while we sat in the living room making love. I just couldn't get enough of this woman. Suddenly Joan said, "Do you smell something?" I jumped off the sofa with my pants around me ankles and yelled. "It's the ham. It's burning. We forgot to check the ham."

As I got up off the sofa, I tripped over my pans and when Joan got to the kitchen and pulled the ham out of the oven, it was black and crispy.

We both laughed and ordered out for pizza and a few beers. That was our first meal as a married couple.

That was the start of a marriage. I thought that happiness would last for an eternity, until death do us part. I never realized that our relationship would come to a bad end. Never.

50

FRANK GETS MARRIED

A year after our wedding, I would be attending another family wedding, that of my brother Frank. That's right, Frank finally married Maria. They had to hire more office help and construction workers because the business was rapidly growing.

A few months after Joan and I returned from honeymoon, we both went to work at our respective schools. I learned to successfully manage unruly students better than I thought I would. I also received a great deal of support from some of the older and more experienced teachers. And of course, Joan was a great help and a source of support.

Once we were at home from school, we would share our experiences about each of our respective schools.

One Saturday evening Joan and I just sat down to enjoy supper when the phone rang. I said, "Wouldn't you know it, just as we sat down, somebody has to Interrupt our dinner. Just ignore it Joan. They can call back at another time."

Joan said. "You better get it Greg. It might be something important."

I sighed and said. "Okay."

I got up from my chair and went to the phone. Annoyed I said. Hello."

"Greg. It's Frank. Can you get out of the house for a few hours?"

I was puzzled, as to why would he ask me to go out alone with him. When we did get together, it was always with Joan and his girlfriend, Maria. "I guess so. How comes brother? What's up."

He didn't tell me why he wanted to meet with me and was very insistent about getting together. "Can you get away? I want to talk to you in person. Not over the phone. It's important."

"Okay but let me finish supper."

"That's fine. See you in a bit."

I yelled out to Joan. "Hey honey, it's Frank. He wants me to go out for a few drinks. He has something he wants to talk about."

"What's that?"

"He won't tell me."

I left the house and met him at a lounge in Cambridge, where we We ordered a few beers.

Frank was acting rather strange. He was clearly anxious about something. "Greg. Good to see you."

As we were drinking our beers I said. "So, what's the big secret? Why all the mystery?

With some hesitation he replied. "Okay, here's the deal. I want to take the big step and get married."

I was shocked. Very surprised. My brother getting married? "Wow. Now that's a real surprise. That's great. When?"

He cleared his throat. "Well, I haven't asked her yet. I don't know. My life has always evolved around you and mom but this would be a big step for me. I don't know? What do you think? How do you like married life?"

I laughed. "Frank. Give me a break. I just got married. This is a new game for me as well. I will say I love it. No more having to go out on dates. Wondering if she loves me or not."

"Let me ask you this, do you still love Joan?"

I laughed. "Frank, what kind of a question is that? Of course, I still love her. She's my whole life."

"But if I marry Maria, how do you think, it will affect our working together. It's one thing when she's my employee but my wife? Won't that complicate our relationship?"

I again laughed. "Frank. Frank. I don't believe you. It wasn't that long ago, when you were giving me advice on how to date a woman. How to treat a woman. Now you want my advice? The advice of a newlywed?"

He laughed. "I guess so. Maybe it's the jitters, talking crazy."

"Let me ask you one question Frank, do you love her?"

"That's a silly question. She's the best thing that ever happened to me. She's a wonderful woman. Of course, I love her."

"Then buy the dam ring and marry her. If you love her, that's all that matters. And the love between you and her will do the job. Go for it. You won't regret it."

"Next question Greg, what do I do about mom? Should we live in the same house with mom or move out?"

"That's a question I can't answer. You need to discuss it with Maria. See what she has to say. When you get married things do change. You need to make the important decisions like where to live, together."

"Now that makes a lot of sense. Why didn't I think of it?"

I joked "That's because you're not a married man."

The next weekend, he took Maria to a nice restaurant down the North End of Boston and proposed to her. She immediately accepted his proposal.

They began to plan for a small wedding with a limited number of people. It was our family and that of Joan's family and our friends. I was his best man and her close friend Joanna was her Maid of honor. They rented a hall, hired a caterer, and had a DJ. They decided to delay the honeymoon because of the business.

When he asked Maria about living in the house with mom, she saw no problem. She, liked the rest of us, loved mom. They were married within five months of his proposal.

And mom was so excited about having another woman in the house. Mom would not be left alone, to live in an empty house. She loved Maria who she came to know since she worked with Frank.

51

A HOUSE OF OUR OWN

After three years of living in the apartment in such cramped quarters, we decided to make the big move, to buy a house of our own. Since we didn't have a clue as to what was involved in making such a purchase, we decided to ask my brother Frank. One evening, mom invited us over for dinner so that we could talk to Frank. Building houses was a substantial part of his business.

Following dinner, we went into the living room where we approached Frank about a house.

"Frank, Joan and I have decided that we want to buy a house. We have been saving our monies from our paychecks and we feel that we have enough for a down payment. What do you think?"

"I think that's great idea. It's about time. I wanted to approach you two about making a purchase but I felt it was best for you to come to me when you were ready. So, here's what I think. I can build you a brand-new house for cost."

"But Frank that's isn't right. That's your living, building houses."

"Gregory, sometimes you're so ignorant to the facts in life. First, the business was left to the both of us. Secondly and more importantly, you're my brother, my only brother. Get it?"

"I guess so."

"Okay. The first thing you need to do is find a piece of land. The developer that I work with can help you with it. Okay?"

"Sure. Sounds great. How much would the land cost?"

"I can talk to him about giving you a discount. It will be affordable. What kind of a house would you like?"

I tuned to Joan. "What do you think hon?"

"Maybe a cape with three bedrooms. Sound right Greg?"

"Fine by me."

"Next Greg, you have to get approval for a bank loan. That shouldn't be a problem. I know the bank manager. We do a lot of business with him."

I laughed. "You seem to know everyone."

"That's my business brother."

"And Mary, that's how we bought our first house. Frank again was there for me one hundred percent."

Mary again had a puzzled look on her face. "I don't understand Greg. Your life was perfect. Why leave it all?"

"You will. You will. I think it's time for me to leave."

"It seems that you leave, every time you don't walk to talk about something."

"You need to understand, I miss them. It pains me not to be with my family."

And I ran out of her office.

52

FAMILY TIME

I did manage to return for my sessions with Mary. She allowed me to continue my story without discussing my quick departure.

"Joan and I finally made it into a house of our own. I never thought the day would come. Our place seemed monstrous in comparison to our small apartment. And we even had a backyard along with a patio for me to do my grilling. Life was perfect. But something was missing. I realized at that very moment, what was missing, the sound of children. It was now time for us to think about starting a family. Prior to that time, I took precautions not to get Joan pregnant. We were now in pretty good shape financially and we were getting older. I wanted to enjoy my children before I became too old. It was definitely time to start a family. Joan was so busy with work and fixing up the house, that she never mentioned anything about wanting to get pregnant. I was the one who broached approached the subject.

It was a Friday night when I decided to approach Joan with the subject of babies.

I was already home from school when Joan walked through the door. She told me she was going to be late so I had already started supper. When it comes to chores around the house, we both pitched in.

When Joan came through the door, she looked exhausted and drained. She threw her coat over the sofa and dropped on to a chair.

I went over and hugged her. "O, honey, looks like those kids beat you up".

She wasn't a happy camper. "Not the kids, it's some of the other teachers. Just some foolish disagreements over teaching methods. I had this terrible and crazy argument with Melissa."

"Want to talk about it?"

"No. Not at all. I could use a glass of wine and some quiet time."

"Wine? But you never drink wine."

She became irritated with me. "Tonight, I need a glass of wine, if you don't mind. Do you understand me?"

"Okay. Okay, take it easy. Be right back. You want anything to go along with it?"

She raised her voice and said. "Don't you understand Gregory? Just a glass of wine."

I suddenly felt that this was not so good time to talk about babies. I returned to the living room with her wine and sat in a chair opposite to her, reading my paper. Didn't say a word for about thirty minutes as Joan quietly sipped her wine. I could see that visibly all that tension and stress was slowly leaving her body with each sip of wine. The muscles on her face were relaxing along with the rest of her body. I then felt like I had my wife back.

She then replied. "Thank you, Gregory, for being so

understanding and allowing me a few minutes to myself. I needed that."

"Given your state of mind, that was the only thing I could do."

She laughed. "And how was your day?"

"Terrific. The kids were great. I was able to engage them in some good discussion on current day events."

"Happy to hear it."

"Not only that. You won't have to cook. I made supper for you."

She then put her glass of wine on the table, came over and kissed me.

Surprised by her response I said, "Wow, I like that. You should have a glass of wine more often."

She laughed. We went into the kitchen, sat down and enjoyed a quiet dinner. I made her favorite meal, spaghetti and meatballs.

As we were eating, she said, "Honey, this is terrific. Thank you so much."

Now that she was relaxed and was in a good mood, I thought it might be time to talk about babies. "Joan I've been thinking.

With a degree of sarcasm, she said. "Well that's a good thing."

"I mean it. I think we should talk about having a baby. What do you think? We're pretty much settled and have a nice big house, so maybe it's time."

Before I could finish my sentence, she came over and sat on my lap and said. "I think we need to get to work on it tonight."

"I was surprised by her response. "Right now?"

She laughed again. "No, after you finish eating and you do the dishes."

And she wasn't kidding. When we were done eating and I had finished the dishes it was about 8:30. We went upstairs, got undressed and went to bed.

Joan had on a pink laced negligee which complimented her perfect body in every way. I mean, I always thought she was perfect.

Once our naked bodies were under the covers, I started kissing her everywhere and I quietly whispered in her ear. "I love you and I hope our love will last forever."

As we experienced each other's sensuous bodies, I felt like I had made it again, to paradise. The softness of her breasts pressing against me. The gentleness of her kisses.

After our love making, I said, "What do you think Joan?"

"I think we got the job done tonight."

"You're right" and I kissed her and we again made love and again made love. My energy seemed endless.

And we did it. Nine months later, I took her to the hospital.

53

OUR FIRST BORN

Joan had a fairly uneventful pregnancy. Joan had the usual morning sickness but all and all it was a good pregnancy. She refrained from drinking and tried to eat healthy. It was an October evening, when Joan woke me up in a panic. "Greg. Greg wake up. It's time."

I was still half asleep, "What do you mean it's time?"

Then I felt a wetness on my side of the bed.

My body sprang upright and I said. "O my god your water broke."

I jumped out of bed in a panic and then proceeded to trip over me shoes and bumping into furniture. I said. "Okay. Okay. Calm down Joan, I have everything under control."

She laughs. "Me calm down? Me? Get my bag, get dressed and give me a minute to put on some clothes."

When Joan was dressed I picked up her overnight bag, left the house, hopped into the car and I drove like a crazy man to the hospital. When we finally got to the Hospital, I ran to the front desk and said to the nurse. "What do I do?"

She was emotionally cold. To her, I was just another crazy husband and wife having their first child. "Nothing. Just fill out these papers please. You've done enough."

"Should I wait here, pace or do what?"

She firmly replied. "Mr. Byrne, I said fill out these forms and take a seat in the waiting room. Do you understand? We'll let you know what the story is, once we get your wife settled and the doctor examines her."

My anxiety continued to grow. . I said. "Okay, the waiting room. Yes, that's a good idea."

After waiting a few minutes, the nurse finally came into the waiting room. I jumped out my chair and said, "What is it? A boy or girl?"

"Settled down Mr. Byrne, she hasn't had the baby yet."

A concerned look soon covered my face. "Okay, so what's the matter? Is she okay? Nothing is wrong, is it?"

"Please, let me talk for a minute, will you?"

"Okay. Okay."

"She won't be delivering for another two hours or more. You might as well go home. We'll call you when she has the baby."

"Go home? What do you mean Go home? I don't want to go home."

She turned around and walked away saying, "Do what you want. You can wait if you want. That's up to you."

The nurse was right. Joan didn't have the baby for two more hours.

After a long two hours that felt like an eternity, the doctor eventually came through the doors with a smile on his face said, "It's a girl. A beautiful 7 lbs. Baby girl"

I stood there for a few seconds trying to absorb the

news. I was officially a father. I had a baby girl. We had a baby girl.

The doctor broke my dream-like state by saying "Mr. Byrne, did you hear me? You have a baby girl."

"Can I see her doctor?"

"You sure can." And he walked away.

When I walked into the room and saw Joan holding our baby girl, I began to cry. There was my daughter being cradled in my wife's arms. "Wow. We really did it. She's so beautiful."

Joan said "Yes, we do make beautiful babies. Would you like to hold her?"

I started to stutter. "Can I? Hold her?"

"She's your daughter, course you can hold her. You're going to be doing a lot of holding. Here, take her. Don't worry she won't break."

I put her in my arms and looked into her tiny face. She was so fragile like a little doll. Thoughts began to run through my head. *Will I be a good father? What will she become? A nurse or maybe a lawyer. My daughter, will someday be going to her Senior prom, graduating college.*"

Joan interrupted my daydreaming. "Gregory. Gregory are you still with us?"

"Sure. Just thinking about our little girl. That's all."

That morning we called Frank and Maria along with Mom and all of Joan's family. Mom was the first person I called to give her the news. I said "Okay, mom you are now officially a grandmother."

She started to stutter. "But...but"

"No buts about it. Joan just had a baby girl and you are now her grandmother, a Nani. That's who you are Grandmother O'Shea."

There was silence on the other end of the phone.

I said, "Mom are you still there?"

"Gregory, I came to your house with no family and now, not only do I have a family but now I'm a grandmother. I can't begin to tell you how happy this makes me. I can't."

"Mom, you have given so much to us. You are the only mother that Frank and I ever had."

She began to cry.

"Mom, why are you crying?"

"They are tears of happiness. I only wish my husband was here with me to share this beautiful day. He would be so proud like it was his own child and granddaughter."

"I wish I had known him. When you talk about your husband, he sounds like a terrific person."

"He was and would have loved to meet all of you."

"Well, you being a grandmother, you know what that means?"

"What?"

"We'll be needing someone to take care of the baby. Joan and I were wondering if you would mind taking care of her. We definitely will pay you. Joan's mother said she would also help."

She laughed. "You want to pay me for taking care of my granddaughter? Don't be foolish. If you pay me, I won't do it."

"But it's a lot of work."

"Gregory, you know me. Work isn't a problem. I can't wait to take care of the little darling."

"O mom, we really appreciate it. Have you ever cared for a baby?"

"No but I'm a woman. I know how to care for a baby. It's like you kids say, it's part of my DNA."

When I told Joan, that mom was willing to take care for Alison, our baby, she was thrilled.

And the days of the week turned into months and then the months turned into years and before I knew it, that little baby I held in my arms was five years old.

Five years old....

54

A Visit from Larry

The next morning, after my visit with Mary, I was awoken early, by a knocking on our broken door. Nick was still sleep, out cold in a drunken stupor.

As I woke, still feeling groggy, I yelled. "Who is it? Go away."

The door than opened and much to my surprise, Larry was standing there wearing fresh clothing, clean shaven and a shit-eating-grin on his face.

"Larry, what the hell are you doing here? I hope you're still with the program."

Larry laughed. "Of course, I am. Today was my first day of leave from the group home. I thought I might come and visit my friends.

I hugged him. "Larry. Larry. I can't believe it. You look terrific. And it's so nice to see you."

"So, where's Nick?"

"He's over there, sleeping it off"

"Can I wake him up?"

"Not a good idea. I hate to say it Larry but he's

◆224◆

gotten worse. Drinking heavily every day and still getting into fights."

"That's too bad. I like Nick. And he saved my life. I wouldn't be here if it were not for Nick"

"Nothing we can do Larry. That is who he is. But I want to hear about you."

"I've been in a re-training program that they have at the center. What a great program. You won't believe it. I'm learning how to become a pastry chef."

I laughed. "You. A pastry chef? I can't picture it."

"But it's true. When I was a kid at home, I loved to watch the cooking shows. I often thought about doing something, having to do with cooking, especially making desserts. Well, my dream has come true. Can you believe it? Me, a pastry chef? Well not exactly a chef but you know what I mean."

"That's great. And you're, living in a group home? What's that like?"

"There are five of us. We're all recovering alcoholics. Each one of us has chores to do like shopping, cleaning and making meals. There is a person like a supervisor who evaluates us and makes sure we do our jobs and keep sober. Nice guy who is also a recovering alcoholic who went through the program. Great Bunch of guys. Made some more friends but you'll always be my number one friend.

"That's nice of you to say that."

"You know Professor, you always stood by me during my bad times. And all the times you tried to help me. When I ended up in the hospital, you'd come and see me almost every day. I didn't forget that Greg. It meant a lot to me. More then what you'll ever know. But enough about me, how are you doing?"

I shook my head and looked down at the floor. I began thinking that I was way behind Larry in resolving my own problems. "Not much has changed. Same old things. My sessions with Mary get kind of rough at times but it's all good."

"You should try getting into the program that I'm in now"

"I wouldn't qualify. I'm not really an alcoholic. Haven't had even one drink since I started seeing Mary. That's the one thing that is better. I don't drink anymore since I started seeing Mary. So, I guess you can say I'm making some progress."

"And the nightmares?"

"I still have them. But not nearly as bad as they had been when I first came to the factory. My medication has helped a lot. And of course, seeing Mary, has made a big difference in my life.

"That's so good to hear Professor. it sounds like you are getting better."

"I guess so. And someday I'll get back to work. I have to tell you one thing, all these sessions with Mary have me thinking about my family. For the longest time, I blocked them out of my mind but telling my stories to her brought my family back to life. It made me think about how much I miss them. So, the therapy has been good but it has also made me feel bad, at the same time. Just thinking about what I'm missing."

"I know what you mean. I've experienced the same thing. But not that I miss my mother or the kind of life I had with her. I've learned to accept things the way they are. And move on. One of these days I'll try to reach out to my mother again and make amends."

"I'm happy for you Larry. I really am. You've come a long way from being homeless."

"I sure have and loving every minute of it. Thanks again Professor. You know, I have an idea."

What's that?"

"I was thinking that I'd like to take you out for lunch, Maybe next week."

"How are you going to do that? You don't have any money."

"But I have a few bucks. At the training center, we even earn a few dollars. Wouldn't that be a kick? Me taking you out for lunch?"

I laughed. "That's something. I'd love to go out but I'm not exactly dressed for lunch in a restaurant."

"Greg. We won't be going to any place fancy. I was thinking more like Wendy's"

I laughed. "Now that more my style."

"When Nick wakes up, let him know I visited and was thinking of him, will you Professor?"

"I will and again, it was so nice to see my old friend."

Larry with a smile on his face and pride in his voice replied. "Okay, I'll see you next week for the best in food at Wendy's."

I again laughed and said. "I see you've acquired a sense of humor."

"I have, now that life is looking good. I've learned to joke and not take things so seriously. Who knows, one of the days I might own my own bakery?"

"That's all within the realm of possibilities my friend. I have to say Larry, it's always nice to see some-one make it out of the factory, this cesspool of a place. Not many do."

"Your next to exit this shithole. I feel it in my

bones. I will pray for you every night. Keep up the good work."

After he left, I thought about what he said. Maybe I will be the next one to get out of this place. Just maybe.

55

My Daughter's First Dance Recital

I again returned to see Mary. And I now felt hopeful that I could make it. Why not? If Larry was able to do it, why not me.

My daughter, Alison, was now five years old. She was a very playful, happy child, who was a regular chatter box. She loved to talk but more than talking, she loved to dance. Alison had been taking dance lessons since she was three. This past year she took lessons twice a week. She was always a part of the larger dance troop thus she never had an opportunity to dance solo. She would be making her first solo performance that evening. Alison was so determined thst she would faithfully practice her routine every day, twice a day and sometimes three times a day. I thought I would lose my mind continuously hearing her dance number over and over again. But I appreciated her determination and perseverance.

Alison always approached everything with enthusiasm

and determination, whether it was dance, school or playing games with her friends. In many ways, she was like her mother. When Joan started a project, she worked hard until she completed it.

Joan had purchased Alison a new costume for the occasion. My daughter was thrilled at having her own unique costume, a costume of her very own.

The night of the dance she said to me. "Daddy, we should go. It's almost 5:00 o'clock."

I was in the living room relaxing, reading my paper. "But Alison, it's only 4:30, we have plenty of time. You don't have to be there until 5:30. It only takes us fifteen minutes to get to the studio"

That was not good enough for my daughter. She responded. "I know daddy but I don't want to be late. You know. There might be a lot of traffic or something." Whenever I go into a discussion with my daughter there was always a But Daddy.

Joan, who was in the kitchen, laughed as she heard our daughter trying to convince me to leave early.

How could I say no my daughter? "Sure, honey get your costume and we'll go."

I truly enjoyed dance recitals when our daughter was performing but to sit through three and four-year old's, attempting to dance, was painfully boring. But I never let my feelings be known to Alison or her mother

I finally gave in to her and said. "Okay honey, we can leave now just in case there's a lot of traffic." She ran over, hugged and kissed me. Her kisses and hugs were the frosting on the cake.

Joan jokingly said. "I can see that you're an easy mark for our daughter. That whatever she wants, she gets from you."

"Joan what can I do?"

She was right, it was next to impossible for me to deny anything my daughter asked for. She would just tilt her head and those eyes would make me melt. I couldn't say no.

When we got to the studio, just as I predicted, we were the first of the parents to arrive.

Mrs. Kelly, the dance instructor, greeted us and said "Well isn't that nice, you're early, very early. Alison, have you been practicing your routine?"

Alison proudly said, "Every day. I'm going to be great."

I turned to Joan and said, "Nothing like having plenty of confidence."

Joan later took Alison, back stage, to change into her costume. At about 5:00 o'clock, the other dancers and their parents flooded the dance studio.

We took our seats in the front row, which was one advantage of getting there early. Before long, Frank, Maria and mom joined us.

Mom was very excited about seeing Allison. She never missed a dance recital. Of course, she had become very close to Alison. She lived with mom when we were working. Alison loved her. Mom had become her second mother.

Once all the parents were settled in their seats, Mrs. Kelly came on to the stage and introduced herself and talked about the evening's program. Once she finished and I made it through seven kiddie acts, my daughter made her entrance on to the stage. The music played and Alison went into her routine. I hate to brag but her routine was perfect. All those days of practicing paid off.

Once she finished, the audience's applause brought a big smile over my daughter's face along with the rest of her family. At the end of the performances, Joan presented her with a stuffed animal and a bouquet of flowers. Mom had also purchased a locket on a gold chain for her. It was a perfect night.

Dancing was not her only accomplishment. Alison was very competitive in the classroom. She always strived to do her best. And when she turned six, she wanted to join the town soccer team along with doing her dancing. We thought it might be a little too much for her but she insisted on doing both activities. We agreed to her demands as long as she kept up her school work. She didn't disappoint us. Alison was such a spark, a well-rounded little girl, who had much potential. We were very proud of her.

I miss her terrible. I often think of her, as I lay in my cot at the shelter. I wondered what she was doing now. Whether she was still playing soccer. Whether she still loved dancing. I wondered what had become of my little angel. I wondered until I fell asleep and my thoughts of my little princess faded.

56

A KILLING

I woke up at the shelter, looking forward to a good breakfast and later in the afternoon going to lunch with my friend Larry at Wendy's. I was in unusually good spirits. Following breakfast, I went to the factory to hang out with Nick. But when I got there; Nick was gone. It was not unusual for him to leave early so I didn't think much of it. I got out one of the books that I had taken from the shelter and decided to read. It was about 11:30, when I left for lunch to meet Larry. When I got there, Larry was already waiting for me at one of the tables, sipping on a cup of coffee. I immediately noticed the proud look on his face. It was if he was treating me to a meal at fine Boston restaurant.

He got up from his chair and greeted me with a hardy handshake. He said. "Hey buddy, I got here a little early so I thought I would grab myself a coffee."

I said, "This is so weird, going to a restaurant with you Larry. I like it. Maybe someday I can return the favor."

"You better pal, especially after all the money I will be putting out for you with this meal."

We bought laughed at what he said.

"I only have until 1:30 Professor since I need to get back to the training center."

"That works for me." I jokingly said, "You know Larry, I also have a busy schedule. I was just able to squeeze you into my long list of appointments." This brought about another round of laughter. It felt really good to be able to joke, especially since there wasn't much humor in my life.

"Well Professor, let's get ordering."

It was fairly crowded. We were about the fourth people in line, ready to place our order.

"Professor, it's on me, so order whatever you want. I mean it. It will be a good break form the food at the shelter."

"Okay. I think I'll have a cheese burger and fries."

"That's it? Why don't you add a cup of chili and a coffee?"

"Are you sure?"

"I'm paying pal. I'm sure."

We placed our orders and continued talking until it was time for Larry to get back to the center. I had one of the best times I ever had since being homeless. It felt like things were normal again.

I left Wendy's and I went back to the factory. When I got there, I saw that Nick was still laying on the floor with a blanket wrapped around him. The few chairs we had in our space were broken and tossed on the floor. It looked like there was a fight. Didn't surprise me. Nick probably got into a fight with someone.

I yelled out to him saying, "Nick what the hell are

you doing in the sack. You know its 2:00 in the afternoon." I yelled again for him to get up but no answer. Now I was beginning to get nervous. "Nick come on, don't play games with me. Man, you must have really tied one on." Still no response.

I went over to get him up when I couldn't believe my eyes. A bloody knife laid next to him. I picked it up and quickly tossed it back on the floor. When I turned him over, I could see the blood oozing from his gut. The blanket that he was laying on, was soaked with blood. I put my fingers next to his neck but there was no pulse. Nick was dead. Someone had killed him. Nick had gotten into one too many fights.

I ran out of the factory in a panic screaming like a mad man. "Help. Help." I finally flagged down a passing police car that was passing bye.

The policeman rolled down his window. I could immediately see that he was annoyed by a homeless man yelling at him. The officer rolled down his window and shouted at me. "So, what do you want buddy?" He sarcastically said. "If you're looking for booze, I don't have any."

"Officer, you have to come with me. My buddy is dead. Someone killed him. He was murdered."

"I think you've been drinking too much." He started to roll up the window when I pounded on the car. "What the hell's the matter with you? I mean it. There's blood all over the place. He's dead. I tried to get a pulse but he has none."

The other policeman in the car, who was driving then turned to him and said. "Maybe we should check it out Mickey."

"Okay pal, where is he? This buddy of yours."

"In the factory. Please come with me. I'll show you."

Still feeling annoyed, he shouted at me. "What do you mean the factory? What the hell are you talking about?"

"O shit, the old factory where most of the homeless hang out" I pointed to the building. He drove to it and parked out in front.

Once inside the building, I took them where poor Nick's body laid.

The first policeman named Micky, carefully picked up the knife with a handkerchief. He held the knife in his hand and then pointed to me. "Is this your knife?"

"No. Of course not."

He then looked down at my hands where I held the knife and said. "Is that blood on your hands?"

"Yes. I just wasn't thinking when I picked up the knife. I didn't mean to disturb your crime scene."

The other cop called the precinct to report the murder and asked them to send help.

The officer named Mickey then said to me. "I think you better come with me."

"Why? You don't think I did this?"

He became angry at my resistance to follow him. "Don't give me a hard time. Just come with me down to the station. We can try and sort this whole mess out."

I didn't want to go with them. I was just reporting the death of my dear friend. "Bu...."

The officer again became angry. "Don't make it hard on yourself. You want to come easy or do you want to do it the hard way?"

I acquiesced to his demands. I had no choice

Once we were at the station, they took me into an interrogation room and a detective by the name of

John Rocca began asking me questions. He began by asking me my name. "What's your name?"

"Gregory Byrne. Am I being accused of Nick's murder?'

"No. You're a person of interest. We are just trying to figure out what happened to him. Did you know the deceased?"

"Yes, I did. He was a good friend of mine. We stayed at the factory, living together. Why would I want to kill my friend?"

"I don't know. Maybe you got into a fight with him."

"I've had my disagreements with him over trying to get him some help. That's what we would fight about. Lately, he was drinking more and more and always getting into fights."

"What was his name?"

"I only knew him as Nick."

"He was a good friend of yours and you only knew him as Nick?"

"Come on detective. He was a homeless guy like me. We don't go into much detail about ourselves." I was becoming angry and thought it was time to get some help. I didn't like the way this was going. "Aren't I entitled to one phone call?"

"Yes you are. But were not accusing of murder. Do you feel you need to make a call?"

"Yes. I feel I need to. I don't like what's going on here."

The detective went into the other room and brought me a phone. I decided to call the only person I knew, Mary.

When the phone began ringing, I was hoping that she would pick it up. It continued to ring but no one was picking it up. I was becoming very nervous thinking *what if she went out? What if she wasn't in the office?*

Finally, she picked up the phone. "Hello Mary, I am so glad to hear your voice."

She could hear the panic in my voice. "What's going on Gregory?"

"I'm in big trouble. I need your help."

"What kind of trouble are you in?"

"I paused before saying the words which got stuck in my throat. "Nick is dead and now the police have me down at the station. They're asking me a lot of questions."

I could hear the disbelief in her voice. "What? Nick is dead? You're at the police station?"

"Yes. He was murdered and I think the police think I killed him. You know me Mary, the last thing I would do is kill someone. Can you help me?"

"O my God. Sit tight Gregory. We have a lawyer on call at the shelter. Give me a while and we'll come down there. In the meantime don't say another word. Do you hear me?

"Thanks. What a relief."

The detective said to me. "I assume you have a lawyer coming down to the station."

"Yes. This conversation is over until my lawyer gets here."

"You sure that's what you want to do?"

"Positive."

The detective called one of the officers, who placed me in a cell until my lawyer and Mary arrived at the station.

Once my lawyer walked through the door, I

experienced a sense of deep relief. My lawyer was a woman in her thirties, by the name of Margaret Cronin. It didn't take her very long to obtain my release since they weren't charging me with murder.

As a result of the murder, all the homeless were evicted from the factory. They owner of the property hired a guard to ensure that they would never again claim the factory for their home. I along with all the homeless, took to the streets, and found rest in entry-ways, and in the Common. I spent most of my days at the Commons and when it was cold, I would seek refuge in an entry way or a sidewalk grill and on occasion I would buy a cup of coffee at one of the fast food places like McDonald's or Burger King. Fortunately, in the evEning, I had a warm comfortable bed at the shelter.

The eviction from the factory brought about a sense of lonliness. When I looked at myself in the mirror, I saw despair. I felt like I was the only one in the world. I wanted to kill myself. I no longer felt that life was worth living. People were dying around me. I needed to talk to Mary. I desperately needed to talk to Mary.

57

ON THE STREETS

Since we could no longer stay at the factory, I began to wander the streets of Boston. I was feeling very depressed. I desperately needed to see Mary. It was late about 4:30 in the afternoon. I didn't know if Mary would be at the shelter since she generally left for home at 4:00pm.

As I walked through the door of the shelter, I thankfully spied Mary about to exit the building. When I saw her, I yelled, "Mary I know you're on your way home but I need to see you."

She paused for a few seconds and with some hesitation said. "Well Gregory. I...I don't know. I was going home to get ready to go out with a friend of mine."

"I'm so sorry to ask you this but I need to talk to someone. You're the only one left. Please."

She kindly responded to my distressed plea and said. "I guess. Let's go back to my office. I first need to make a call."

"Thank you. Thank you."

We went back to her office where she called her

date and said, "Tommy, I hope you don't mind but something has come up. Why don't we push up dinner to 6:30?" There was a pause before she said. "O thank you. You're a doll. Love you to."

Mary then turned to me and said. "Gregory. You look terrible. What's happening? What is so urgent that it couldn't wait until next week?"

"My world is gone. Nick is Dead. Mac is dead. The factory is closed. I know it's not much but it was my world. I'm just feeling low. I mean." My sadness had overcome my being so that I had trouble describing my feelings.

Mary suddenly grew very serious. "Are you having thoughts of suicide?"

I broke down and cried. "I don't want to live anymore. I really don't. Everybody I love is dying around me. I screwed up my family, the family that I love. Nick was murdered. I know we had our differences but he was a body, somebody I could talk to when he wasn't drunk. His death just put me over the top. I screwed up again. I should have done something to prevent his death, his murder." I began to cry uncontrollable.

Mary in her own compassionate way tried to comfort me. "Gregory. Listen to me. Nick was on a road to destroy himself. Nobody could have prevented what happened. You yourself said, he was getting into more fights and was drinking more."

"I guess. I don't know anything anymore."

"Gregory, you are a good caring guy. If you weren't so caring and loving, you wouldn't be so upset. You can't save the world. Do you hear me? Tell me Gregory, do you want to go to a hospital?"

"No. No hospitals. I just need you."

She then began to yell. "Gregory. You need to look at

what you've accomplished. You are better. You stopped drinking that is a major accomplishment. Not many homeless men can do what you've done. And you are making progress in our session. Gregory focus on the positives."

The more she talked the better I began to feel.

"Tell you what Gregory, I'm going to give you my personal number. If you ever, ever feel like you want to talk, if you feel like you are going to kill yourself. Feeling real down. Call me. And tomorrow I want you to come in to see the doctor. That's not negotiable. He can give you something for your present depressive state. Will you do that?"

"I will Mary. I will. And again, thank you for being there for me."

"Keep working on your problems until you again regain your life.

I have a lot of faith in you Gregory. Your family needs you. The world needs people like you, people who give a dam. Start believing in yourself. You have a lot to offer. Do you hear me? Do you?" she shouted.

"I'll try."

"Now grab something to eat from the kitchen and try to have a restful sleep. See you on Monday."

"I will. And I'm sorry for interrupting your evening and date."

Mary laughed. "Tom knows that if he dates me, he has to put up with my work, my job. He really is a good guy, just like you."

"He's one lucky guy."

I did get some food from the kitchen and slept better that night. If I didn't have Mary, I might have taken my life. I went to see the doctor the next day and he gave me an anti-depressant that helped.

58

A NEW FAMILY MEMBER

My daughter, Alison, had become the center of attraction for all of us, especially mom. Alison had adopted my mother, as her second mom and my mom happily accepted the honor of being more than just a grandmother. When Alison wasn't dancing or playing soccer, she would be spending time with my mom, who patiently taught her how to cook and sew. They would make doll clothes together. Yes, dolls were still very much a part of her life. The two of them, Alison and mom were inseparable.

When Alison played soccer, mom would happily drive her to soccer practice. She loved to go to her games. She never missed a game. When at the field, I think my mom was the most vocal, cheering the team on. And of course, whether they won or lost a game, it was always ice cream for Alison. Joan would sometimes become angry with mom saying that the ice cream would spoil her dinner but mom just ignored her and continued the tradition of taking the kids for is cream. When she asked if some of her friends could come, mom would end up paying for four or five of the young ladies.

Frank and Maria, became Alison's uncle and aunt. They loved her since she brought joy to everyone. She gave life to a world that was desperately in need of love. There were times when my brother and Maria would ask her to sleep over their house. They would make popcorn and watch a Disney movie.

The sight of Alison and the happiness she brought to all of us, prompted Frank to invite Joan and I over their house for dinner and of course Alison also came with us.

Once we finished eating, we remained in the kitchen while Alison went into the living room to watch television.

Frank and Maria had been trying to have a child of their own for years with no success. They badly wanted to have children and now with Alison in their lives, their desire was increased tenfold.

While we sat around the kitchen table having coffee, Frank said, "Maria and I have been thinking about adopting a child. Maria said after seeing Alison and how much life she has brought to the whole family, we can't wait anymore to have children of our own."

Frank said. "Plus, we're getting older and we want to enjoy our children while we still have energy and are able."

Joan said, with a smile, "I think that's great idea. Both of you would make excellent parents."

I then said, "So Frank, what's the problem?"

Frank shook his head. "To say the least, we have some reservations."

"Like what?"

"What if the child turns out to be a problem. We don't know where these kids come from, what their parents are like. And why would a woman give up a child?"

"I would agree that those are legitimate concerns but millions of parents have adopted and things have worked out. Look at us? We turned out pretty good, in spite of our crazy mother.

Frank laughed. We continued to discuss the pros and cons of adoption and finally Maria turned to Frank and said, "That's it Frank, where going to do it."

Frank was clueless as to what to do. "But where do we go?"

Maria with a smile on her face said, "Well I have to admit that I've been looking into it. I had explored several agencies and I think we should go with Catholic Charities."

Frank laughed. "You son of a gun and when were you going to tell me?"

"In time, I was going to tell you but I thought it would be best for you to see what other people thought of the idea especially your own brother and sister in law. We had talked about it before but you never seemed to be keen on the idea."

I then turned to my brother and said. "So, what do you think Frank?"

Frank sighed and then yelled, "Hell, why not?"

The very next day Maria didn't waste any time making an appointment with the Adoption agency.

The agency did a thorough background check and they were approved for adoption. The odds of getting a newborn were very slim, especially in light of Frank and Maria's age.

They waited patiently for a call and eventually a woman from the agency called them. The woman at the agency, a Mrs. Abigail Murray said that they have a Korean boy about age 10. Frank and Maria immediately fell in love with him even before they got a chance to meet him.

They flew to Korea and Daniel became part of their family.

Alison was so excited about having a cousin. She took pride in helping him to adjust to the American ways of life.

And Maria spent her days working at home in one of the bed rooms that was converted into an office. Frank hired another woman to supplement Maria's work.

And mom, well mom accepted the challenge of having another child to tend to. She spent every day, teaching him English. And she also learned how to make Korean dishes, especially for Danny.

In time Danny joined Alison in playing soccer.

Our families were not complete. But almost complete.

59

THE STORY CONTINUES

Alison was now six years old when Joan approached me. "Gregory, I think it's time for our daughter to have a brother or sister."

"What do you think?"

"I love the idea. Why don't we get to work on it right away."

"Come on Frank, be serious."

"Okay. I am serious, very serious. I was thinking about the same thing for a while. But one problem, we can't expect mom to care for another child. We'll have to hire a nannie or someone to take care of the baby."

"No, I don't our baby to be raised by a stranger."

"But what else can we do?"

"I was thinking of taking a few years off until the new born is in school. What do you think?"

I grimaced. "Joan, that's going to be kind of tight on just one paycheck coming into the house."

"I know it but it will be worth it. We can manage. Maybe I can get a part-time job in the evening at a department store of something."

"Well Joan, if you don't mind cutting a few corners and living on a tighter budget, we can give it a try."

"oan ran over and kissed me. "Greg, you're the best."

Once she became pregnant, she immediately let her parents know and I told my family. Mom was very happy for us. She became excited over the thought of caring for another child but was disappointed when we told her that Joan was taking a leave of absence from work to care for the baby. We assured her that there would be plenty of opportunities for her to help out. And there were. Mom gave Joan a chance to do errands, housecleaning and other things.

Joan had a fairly easy pregnancy except for the first few months with morning sickness. Alison loved to touch her belly once she began to show. She couldn't wait to have her own baby sister or brother, but mostly, she was hoping for a sister, so that she could be the older sister. The doctor had given her a clean bill of health and said she had no problems having babies.

It was in June on the 19th that I was at home watching television, when Joan began to have contractures.

It was 10:00 in the evening. Alison was sound sleep. Joan turned to me and said. "Gregory, the contractures are coming closer. I think you better call someone to stay with Alison. We need to go to the hospital.

I suddenly became wide awake. "Okay, I'll give Frank a call."

When Frank picked up the phone he said, "Hey brother, what are you doing calling at this hour? Everything all right?"

"No, I think Joan is going to have the baby. Could you come over the house and stay with Alison?"

I'll be right there. When Frank walked through the

door, Joan's water broke. I put her in the car along with some luggage she had already prepared in case of an emergency, and it was an emergency.

We quickly drove to the hospital, filled out the necessary papers, and I waited patiently.

It seemed like such a long night, before the doctor walked through the swinging doors and said, "Well my son, you have a baby boy."

My eyes seemed to be popping out of their sockets when I heard it was a boy. "Did you say boy doc?"

"I sure did."

"Can I see my wife and the baby now?"

"Go right ahead. They're waiting for you.".

When I walked into the room and saw my son for the first time being held in my wife's arms, it caused me to have goose bumps. A boy.

Cheerfully Joan said. "Hi honey, so what do you think of your son?"

"Wow. He looks much bigger than Alison."

"He sure is, weighing in, at 8 lbs. 3 ounces. Greg, why don't you hold him?"

I gently took him from Joan's arms and said. "Hey big guy, welcome to the Byrne's family. You're going to like it here with Alison and Danny."

As I held him in my arms and rocked him, I said to Joan, "And how are you doing Joan?"

"Actually, I'm feeling pretty good for delivering such a big baby.

"What will we name him Joan?"

"I was thinking about Christopher. What you think?"

"Hey Chris how do you like your new name?"

We both laughed.

Joan looked at me and said. "Honey, it's been a long night. Why don't you go home and you can let the family know tomorrow?"

"Okay. Here you go Chris, back to your mother's arms." I gave him back to Joan and gently kissed her. "I love you Joan. I love our family. Thank you for everything. The best thing that ever-happened to me was the day I met you."

"And I love you to Greg. Now maybe it's time that we all get some rest."

I didn't sleep much that night with the excitement of another baby.

Mary said. "When you talk about your past and your family it sounds like it was the best time in your life. Just about every time you talk about your family, you glow with happiness."

"They were such good years." I got up from my chair and left her office.

60

A Son

The birth of my son brought about another new dimension of happiness. Alison soon became his second mothers. She loved to feed him and mom couldn't wait to get her hands on him. Alison and mom took turns caring for him whenever possible. And of course, Danny, Frank's son, joined in as part of the caring brigade. It was a wonderful and happy times.

When Chris turned five, my brother Frank came to me and said. "Greg, I have a great idea, why don't we take them all to Disneyland in Florida. You know the kids have been talking about it for the past few months."

"You mean everyone, mom included?"

"I mean everyone. It will be a blast."

"I think it would be a great idea but money is limited in our house, you know what I mean?"

"Not a problem, you own part of this business, so we'll take it out of the business."

"That's very generous of you Frank but...."

"No buts about it. It's done. Wait till the kids hear about this. They'll go ballistic."

The next day, we told the kids and they were very excited. At first, they thought we were kidding but then soon realized that we were dead serious about going. Our plan was to go Disney in August before the start of school.

When I told mom that we wanted her to come with us, she said, "No. I'm too old. You young people go. I don't need to go to Disney"

"Mom, have you ever been there?"

"No. I didn't go to many places with my husband."

"Well now is your chance to make up for all the traveling you never did."

When the kids heard me trying to convince mom to go with us, they all came over and yelled at her saying, "You have to go. It won't be any fun without you."

She began to laugh. "I'm too old."

"No, you're not nannie, we want you to come."

She suddenly burst into laughter." I don't know."

They all said in unison, "Please?"

"Okay I go.".

The kids yelled so hard, when mom agreed to go with them, that I thought the roof was going to come off the house.

We boarded a plane to Florida in late August with plans to stay for a week. Frank and Maria made all the plans and hotel accommodations. We stayed on the grounds at Disney's.

The flight was the first time that mom had ever been on a plane. She was scared but the kids surrounded her with Alison on one side and Danny on the other, they held her hands as the plane took off. Mom was absolutely petrified as the plane left the runway. She kept her eyes closed until we were in flight and then she let go of her breathe.

That week, the kids dragged mom to every ride with a few exceptions. This was her first real vacation. The kids laughed and were scared to death on some ride, ate lots of pizza and ice cream and mom love to see the expression on their faces as they ran from one ride to another and one show to another show.

61

SOCCER

Soccer had taken over our lives. Once Chris saw the other kids going to soccer practice and watching the games, he decided that he didn't want to be left out. We signed my son up to play town soccer. He loved playing the game but he also made tons of friends. Our house had become like a gas station with kids coming and going and refueling with mom's cookies and brownies. There were also a multitude of sleepovers between Chris and Alison.

Chris didn't have any trouble learning the game. He had two excellent teachers and coaches between Alison and Danny. When they had spare times, which was not very often, they would teach him all the moves and how best to play the game. Our backyard became filled with the happiness with neighbor kids and family. Our yard became the central meeting place for the neighborhood kids.

When possible, Frank and I would go to an the afternoon as many soccer game. But the real soccer mom, was our mother. We had bought a van to transport the children with all their gear to the games. Mom would frequently be the driver. She loved spending time with her grandchildren. She slowly learned the game and before long was acting as their coach in the backyard.

During the games, you could hear mom yelling and screaming for the home team. After the first year of their playing, she was voted by the school as the number one soccer fan. They held a little ceremony on the fields and she was given a soccer ball with all the young players signing it. Our children were proud very prou-dof her.

I don't think there was absolutely nothing that mom couldn't do, from cooking to cheerleader to soccer coach. She became the talk of the town. In many ways she was a town celebrity. She couldn't walk throughout a store without someone talking to her and of course, all the kids from the little ones to the older ones, loved her special chocolate chip cookies.

As a family, we couldn't have been happier.

And then it happened on a cold December night. Something that forever changed our family.

62

A Stoke of Bad Luck

On quiet Sunday evening in March, Joan, the children and I were watching a Disney movie. I made some popcorn and entered the living room where the kids were glued to the show.

"Here we go, popcorn for everyone. I made two patches, so help yourself."

Joan got up and said, "I'll get us some drinks."

Joan left the room and went into the kitchen to get the drinks.

The kitchen phone rang and Joan said, "I'll get it honey.

"Thanks. If it's for me, I'm not here. This is my night to enjoy this great movie with my family." I turned to my two children and said. "This is going to be a good one."

Alison said, "quiet dad. No talking. Go into the other room if you want to talk."

"Sorryyyyyy."

I took a handful of popcorn and was about to put it into my mouth, when Joan said, "Greg, it's your brother Frank. He sounds upset."

"I'll be right there."

"Hey Frank what's up?"

"Bad news Greg."

"O my God, what happened?"

"The ambulance just took mom to the hospital. I think she might have had a stroke. I'm going to a make a run over there, do you want to come with me?"

"I'll take my own car and meet you there."

When I got there, Frank was already in the waiting room. When he saw me, he hugged me and said. "I'm Glad I caught you home."

"So, what happened?"

"She was in the kitchen cleaning up the dishes and having a cup of tea when I heard this loud crash. I ran into the kitchen and found her laying on the floor, surround by broken dishes. I tried to talk to her but she didn't respond. I immediately called 911 and here we are."

As I started to talk, I became visibly upset. My breathing became labored and I began to shake my heads in disbelief. I turned to Mary and said, "Sorry Mary, I have to leave."

Mary became angry, and quickly responded by saying. "No Greg you're not going to leave. Not again. Dam it all Greg, every time you relate an upsetting incident in your life you run away. You need to face your feelings. No more running. Do you hear me?"

I never heard her speak that way to anyone. She completely took me by surprise.

Mary continued. "Running away from your problems stops now.

You will begin to deal with your feelings and your past now or you'll be homeless for the rest of your life. Do you hear me Mr. Byrne?"

I tried to respond. "But....."

"No buts about it. Now"

I began to stutter. "I...Don't know...I

"You do know."

While my head looked down at the floor, I sighed

"Tell me what you're feeling right now. Tell me Greg or this session and all future sessions are over."

I started to angrily shout at her. "You want to hear about my feelings? You want to hear about my past/I'll tell you. It was happening to me again, first my dad died. The most important person in my life, died. I loved him and he loved me." My eyes began to fill with tears. "And now the only mother I ever had looked like she was going to die. You want to know what I'm feeling? Empty. Dam it all; empty. Darkness. Like the lights in my life had gone out, that's what I felt like on that day. You satisfied now? Are you?"

"Yes I am. Those feelings were a long-time coming Gregory."

"Maybe but I shouldn't be taken t it out on you."

"Gregory, you have every right to those feelings. Life has not been kind to you. Those dark feelings have been festering in you all those years. Building up in you, like a time bomb."

I guess you're right. She is the only mother I had. I didn't want to lose her."

"I can readily see that, but what happened to your mom?" Did she die?"

63

MOM

The doctor final came out to meet us. I had never seen Frank so upset about mom. We didn't know what would become of her. We introduced ourselves to him and I said, "Is she going to be all right Doctor?"

He sighed, before answering my question. "I think she is but I'm not sure how much of her functioning she will be able to recover at her age. Her age is against her. She has a lot of rehab in front of her. We will get her some physical therapy, and speech therapy. But for now, she'll be using a wheelchair to get around. I really don't know if she will be able to walk without the help of a walker or at the very least a cane. She has suffered left sided paralysis."

"What does that mean?"

"Her paralysis is on the left side which means it will affect her speech her walking and the use of her arms. I believe, that with help, she will be able to talk again."

"What happens to her now?"

"She will be sent to a nursing home for her rehabilitation We will initiate her rehab here at the hospital."

"How long before she can come home?"

"That's a tough question to answer. We want her to be functional, that is being able to get around on her own. It might take a good month or so. Depends upon how much progress she makes."

"Can we see her?"

"Sure but she's unconscious at the moment. I needed to give her a sedative."

We both went into her room, and saw poor mom laying in her bed. She had never been sick in all the years we've know her. Not even a cold could slow her down. This very active vibrant woman who was always doing for someone, now she laid helplessly in bed.

I tried talking to her. "Hey Mom. Your boys are right here. We're going to get you better again; the kids need you and we need you. So, you better get better quick."

When Frank began to speak tears started to stream down the side of his face. He then approached her, held her hand which lay limp on the bed and gently kissed her on the cheek. This was not the frank I had known. He was always the rugged macho man, nothing ever bothered him.

I said goodbye to Frank and we both returned home.

When I walked through the door, Joan greeted me along with the children whose eyes were red from crying.

Joan said, "They didn't want to go to bed until you came home. They were crying most of the evening and......"

Before she could finish her sentence, I gathered my family together and we hugged each other.

The children then said, "Is nani going to be okay daddy. Is she?"

"Yes. When I left her, she was resting peacefully?"

"What happened Daddy?"

"She had a stroke."

Alison said. "What's that?"

I explained the idea of a stroke as best I could and said that she wouldn't be home for a while. The people at the nursing home will be getting her better.

The children again began to cry and we hugged them tightly.

64

THE CHILDREN VISIT

O ur children including Frank's and Marie's Danny wanted to see their precious nani. We said that they couldn't see her until she got a little better.

They reluctantly accepted our decision to delay their visit with disappointment. Mom had become a very important part of their lives.

Mom started her long journey to recovery at the Crescent Nursing Home and rehab center in Arlington. It was a long grueling rehabilitation but she was a strong woman with much determination. She wasn't going to allow something like a stroke from keeping her from her family and taking on her role as the family Matriarch.

After a week and a half at the center, we decided that it was time for the children to see her. Mom was showing some signs of recovering in her speech and they were beginning to have her walk short distances. Each day she began to gain some of her strength.

We decided that we didn't want all of us to invade the center so my family and children were the first to see her.

When the children walked into the dayroom, mom was in a comfortable chair with a wheelchair at her side looking out the window, When she saw the children, she began to grin and smile and held out her arms to welcome Alison and Chris. The children immediately ran over to her and began hugging her, yelling, "Nani. Nani."

Mom tried talking but the words wouldn't leave her mouth. Her speech was also garbled. All she could say was "hi. hi." It was clear that she was frustrated by her inability to express herself.

Alison said, "I and Christopher made some cookies for you just like you taught us and we bought you a box of your favorite tea."

As they handled her their gifts, mom could no longer contain her joy and began to cry.

Alison turned to me and said. "Why is she crying daddy?"

"She's crying because she is so happy to see you children. You know how much your nani loves you."

The both of them began to vigorously hug their cherished nani. I said, "Take it easy with the hugs kids."

It was an up-setting experience for all of us but the children were delighted to see her. The next day Frank, Maria and Danny went to see her with a similar response.

All the children insisted on seeing her everyday but we said, we could only do it three times a week since she needed to get her rest and therapies. They seemed to reluctantly accept our explanation.

65

SLOW PROGRESS

H er recovery was slow but she was eventually able to progress to the point of using a walker but she would never walk again on her own. Her speech did improve so that she was able to carry on a conversation but she still struggled to say the thoughts that were in her head. We all accepted her as she was. She also would become very frustrated when she tried to cook since her abilities were compromised by the stroke.

When mom was in the hospital, we needed to make some changes in her household, Frank hired a woman to help with the housecleaning and making the meals. We knew that it would not sit well with mom but it had to be done. As predicted, when mom came home, and saw another woman in her house she was outraged. She insistent that she didn't need any help but she did. It was very difficult for her to accept another woman in her domain. The woman, a Mrs. McAvoy would do her work and leave. She was more than understanding of mom's condition. She could only prepare lunches and supper under the supervision of mom. There were many disagreements with Mrs. McAvoy and mom.

Alison and Chris were frequent visitors to mom's house which delighted her. They would play games with her and she would continue to show them how to make cookies and cake and supervise Alison's sewing lessons.

When it came to our children playing their sports, mom insisted on going to the games as the head cheer-leader for their teams.

The first time she went to their soccer games, every-one in the stands, stood up and gave her a deafening cheer. People greeted her with hugs and kisses from the adults to the children. She had become the unof-ficial Mayor of Arlington.

Yes, I was delighted by her fans' welcome but felt bad that her activities were limited. I could see the disappointment and frustration in her eyes when she couldn't do her previous activities.

Mary said. "I would assume that it was as difficult for you as it was for her to see your mom that way?"

"Yes, it was but you try to make the best of it."

"You do and apparently you did make the best of it. I was wondering Gregory, how is the medication work-ing for you?"

"Pretty good. I'm feeling much better now, thanks to you."

"That's nice to hear. And what are you doing during the day for shelter during the cold weather?

I laughed. "Surviving. I manage to find some warmth and comfort in the department stores. Some of the salespeople have come to know me since I spend a lot of time in the stores. I also spend time in the library, and read."

"You are resourceful Gregory and quite charming with the ladies."

I laughed. "I guess so. I just try to be nice to people when they are nice to me."

"And the nightmares?"

"Some improvement. Much better then when I first came to the shelter."

"Good. So, I'll see you next week?"

"You bet."

I left her office feeling that I was finally making some strides. Mary and the medications were making a difference in my life.

66

THE ACCIDENT

I continued seeing Mary and related how well, the children were doing with their sports and in school. Chris had eventually given up soccer to play baseball which he fell in love with. He dreamed of becoming a profession baseball player. We didn't discourage him. We both felt it was a good idea to have dreams at his age. For that matter, at any age. Time would test the reality of those dreams.

My therapy with Mary soon reached a real critical turning point. I finally was able to talk about the one thing in my life that brought about my homelessness.

Mary began the session by asking me how I was doing. For the very first time in all the months I was seeing her, I brought up my son

"So, Gregory, what's happening?"

I didn't answer her question and instead I suddenly said. "Something happened with my son." I finally found the courage to talk about Chris.

"Something happened with your son? Would you like to tell me about it?"

I took a deep breath and tried to find the words. "Let's see, where do I begin." I hesitated to discuss, what I was about to say. This part of my past was a secret, that I had closely guarded all these years.

"Gregory, take your time."

Emotions over took me. I could hardly get the words out of my mouth. "This is hard. I never told anyone about what happened to my son since I left home."

"Okay. I'm listening Gregory, I'm right here for you. Take your time."

I took another deep breath before I began my life-changing story.

"Well it was in December. The beginning of the month. There was a light covering of snow on the ground." I paused for a few minutes. Mary allowed me my space. Seldom pushed me to talk. "Sorry Mary."

"No need to apologize. I know this isn't easy for you. You're doing good Gregory."

"Okay, where was I? My son Chris wanted to go over his friends' house to play some new video game. His friend wanted him to come for supper and leave early because of the snow. I told Joan, that I would drive Chris."

My wife Joan paused for a few minutes before saying. "I don't think you should go. It's snowing and the roads might become hazardous by the time you bring him home."

Chris hearing our conversation said. "O ma. Please can I go? It's just up the street. There's not much snow in the ground. Please?

Joan shook her head saying. "I don't think so Chris. No."

I looked out the window and saw that the snow

was barely covering the street. I then approached Joan and said. "Come on Joan. I'll be super careful. Chris has been looking forward to this for a week. This video game has finally arrived. Besides, there's not much snow on the ground. I just took a look out the window."

Joan walked away as she threw up her hands in disgust. "You two do as you want."

I went after her. "Joan."

I put my hands on her shoulder and she quickly brushed it away. "No, I don't think you should go. But I'm only his mother. What do I know?"

I did have some reservations about going out that night but I thought it was local, and what could happen?

"Okay Chris, get you jacket and boots on and we'll leave. But I'm going to pick you up right after supper. No later. Do you understand?

Chris was very excited. "I understand dad. Thanks. You're the best."

It was always hard for me to refuse any request from my children. My own childhood was so miserable that I wanted them to have everything that I didn't have.

We drove to his friend's house without a problem. The snow was still coming down but an inch hadn't accumulated on the roads. His friend's house was about five minutes away. I dropped him off and returned home without a problem., It was about 7:00, when I got the call that he was ready for me to pick him up.

I left my house to pick up my son. Once Chris was in the car I said. "So, did you have a good time?"

"O dad, it was awesome. I mean, we had so much fun. Thank you. Can I get one of those games dad.?"

"Someday I'll get you one but not this year. Money is a bit tight.'

"Thanks dad."

I began to stutter as I related my story to Mary I could hardly complete a sentence. "We were about.. O God.....About five... Let me see. About two minutes from home. Than a truck. A dam truck..Shit..The truck hit.. us. It killed... my son. The truck killed my son. I killed him." I started to scream and repeat it. "I killed him Joan. What kind of a father kills his only son?"

Joan came around the side of the desk and put her hands on my shoulder. "Okay Gregory. You're going to make it. You are. Want to break now?"

"No. No. I need to finish this. The next thing I remembered was waking up in the hospital. I didn't know what had happened. My family surrounded me. I began to hear Joan saying "Greg? Greg can you hear me?"

I was still dazed and didn't remember what had happened. "Where am I? What happened?"

Joan softly said. "You're in as hospital there's been an accident." She then began to cry. Joan was so upset that she left my side and went out of the room. She couldn't tell me that my son was dead

"An accident?"

Mary sympathetically moved by my side. "Yes. A terrible accident Greg. A bad accident."

Suddenly, bits and pieces of my memory began to push through into my consciousness. I tried to sit up but my body was so racked with pain, it would not allow me to do anything. I remember now. I was driving Chris home from his friends' house when something hit us and everything went dark. In a panic I said, "O my God. Where's Chris? Is he badly hurt? Is he okay?"

No one said a word. The room went silent.

I began to yell. "Where the hell is my son? I need to see him."

I started to try to get out of bed, when Frank said. "I have some bad news Greg." Frank began to cry. "Chris didn't make it."

I started to cry uncontrollable between my tears, "What do you mean he's dead? Noooo. It can't be."

Frank replied, "Chris didn't make it. I'm sorry Greg."

I started to yell and scream, and punch my face. "I killed my son. I killed my son."

I was so out of control that the nurse came rushing into my room and gave me a sedative to calm me down.

I then stopped talking to Mary. Just looked down at the floor. It felt like I was experiencing my terrible nightmare, only I was awake.

"Greg. You okay?"

"If I had only listened to Joan, Chris would be alive."

I again became very upset and started to cry.

Mary said. "Do you hear me Gregory, it was an accident. You couldn't have known that a truck would skid out of control and hit your car."

"No. I should have, listen to my Joan. She was right. It's happening all over and over. So many people I love are dead like my father. My son. Mac. Nick. And mom is a cripple for life."

"Maybe and only maybe it wasn't the best decision. But you need to realize that people don't always do the right thing all the time but those decisions don't always end up with someone dying. It was just a freak accident. Bad luck. You took your son to his friend's house became you loved him. You did it out of love. You're not God Gregory. You can't control everything." Mary began to yell.

"Maybe you're right Mary but it's hard for me not to feel so guilty."

"Gregory, do you now see what's behind your nightmares?"

"I don't know. I don't know anything anymore."

"Your nightmares are an expression of the tremendous guilt you have been carrying, all those years. You believed that you killed your son and destroyed your family. Does that make sense?"

"I never thought it that way. You might be right."

"There are times when our guilt becomes unbearable, our mind can no longer deal with bad things so it presents itself in the form of a nightmare. Your guilt has robbed you of your life but it also deprived your daughter of a father, your wife of a husband, a brother of a brother and your mom of a son. Did you ever think of what your leaving home has done to your family?"

"No. I was just blinded by my own guilt and grief."

Mary again began to raise her voice so that I would get her message. "Do you really want them to experience the grief of losing you? Do you want them to suffer again, knowing if you are alive or dead? Joan lost a son. Don't let her lose a husband and your daughter a father. Do you?"

"No, I never thought of it that way. It sounds kind of selfish."

"Your wife Joan needed you as much as you needed her Gregory. She was hurting when Chris died. You were not the only one who was feeling such pain over the loss of your son. Everyone was hurting."

"But how can I go back home after all these years? It's too late."

"Greg, it's never too late. You need to go home. They still need you. I can clearly see that you still have a lot more love to give, to your family.

"So, what do I do?"

"Join the human race. I can help you move off the streets and into a group home and then into an apartment. I can get you a job. You can be on your way to life again. What do you think?"

I hesitated for a moment, not saying a word because I was terrified about possibility of reuniting with my family.

"Greg are you with me? Are you willing to try?"

"I'll give it a try. I don't know how I'll do but I'll give it a try."

"Good. I'll start making some calls for you to go to the Work Center. I know they could use you"

"But I thought the program was only for alcoholic."

"You're right. But you'll be going to the center as a worker?"

"As a worker? I can't do anything?"

"But you're a teacher. They need people to help these men get their High School diploma."

"I don't know if I can do it. It's been a long time."

"Come on Gregory. Don't hand me that bullshit. Of course you can do it. You don't forget how to teach. Right now, your feeling anxious but once you get going your anxiety will subside. What do you say?"

"Okay. I'm in. Will I get paid?"

Of course, you'll get a paycheck but initially I want you to apply for welfare."

"I've never been on welfare in all my life."

"So, this will be your first time and probably your last time. It will be short term. Like I said before, I can get you into a group home for now and then you can graduate into your own apartment. Sound good?"

"I guess I have a lot of work to do."

"Dam right you do but you can do it."

"How do you feel now?"

"Overwhelmed."

"Of course, you do but it will be a lot better than spending the rest of your life being homeless and living on the streets."

"I guess so."

"It's only natural to have some reservations about getting your life back on track but you've already taken the first step. Congratulations."

"Okay Mary, I trust you know what you're doing. You seem to have more faith in me than I do in myself."

She laughed. "Your faith will come. Believe me."

"Thanks again for saving my butt."

When I left here office my head was spinning. I wondered if this was really going to happen. Will I be able to get my life back? Will I?

67

The Start of a New Life

That Friday, I returned to Mary as she asked, to get the details of what I would be doing at the center.

"Greg, I first want you to go to the group home today and ask for Mike Sullivan. He runs the home out of East Arlington. Are you familiar with Arlington?

"I Know it well."

"Good. He will get you settled into a room and tell you about the house rules. Than you need to go to the Welfare office and fill out some forms in order to file for financial aid. The worker there is a woman by the name of Marion Higgins. I've already talked to her and she know you're coming."

"What do I do for money right now before I get my first welfare check?"

She then handed me an envelope. "Take this. It will get you started."

"But I can't pay you back."

"You don't have to. We have a kitty at the shelter that we use to help people such as yourself. And on Monday, report to the training center in Boston and see a man by the name of Carl VonBeger. He runs their training program. I already told him about your educational background and he's excited about your coming to the center."

"Wow. You don't waste any time."

"You need to get moving. And one other thing. Take this bag which has some clothes for you to wear. They're not new but they're are much better then what you're wearing. I picked them up for you at the church which receives and distributes clothing to the poor. You qualified."

I reluctantly took the bag. "Why are you doing this for a bum like me?"

"Because you're not a bum. I believe in you, like I said before."

"I won't disappoint you Mary."

"Don't worry about me. Don't disappoint yourself. Okay. any questions?"

"No. I can't tell you how much I appreciate this. Someday I'll pay you back."

I left her office to change into my new clothes. She had also enclosed a set of toilet articles. She didn't forget a thing. Once changed, I was off to the group home.

When I arrived there, I was greeted by the supervisor, who turned out to be a real nice He talked to me about what he expected of me and gave me a list of chores I would be responsible for.

He said "The list will change weekly, so check it."

He also said. "There is a curfew. You need to be home for supper and in bed by 10:00pm. No drinking. No drugs. If you screw up, you'll find yourself on the street." And he meant it.

I than met four of the other guys who all had similar

stories. They showed me my room which I shared with another man, by the name of Tony Marconi, a man in his forties, who use to work as an auto mechanic until his divorce, and his drinking put him on the streets.

We went to lunch and I won the job of doing the dishes at the center. After eating I told Sullivan, that I needed to go to the work center which didn't present a problem. Most of the men attended the center for re-training and to develop marketable skills.

When I got to the center, Carl Von Berger, welcomed me and began by taking down some basic information and my past experiences as a social studies teacher. I expressed my reservation about again teaching since I hadn't taught for some years. He felt that I should give it a try and if it doesn't work out, they would evaluate me for another kind of work. He related to me that this place was basically a training center. He explained that the men are here for job re-training and placement. He said I would be having a class of about of about 10-15 people.

I then returned back to the group center and imme-diately went to my room until supper. I was completely worn out. Emotionally spent.

After supper, I along with the rest of the men, went into the common room to watch a little television and then I turned in early. Tomorrow was another day. I went to the welfare office in Boston and was able to receive some temporary financial aid.

On Tuesday, I held my first class at the training cen-ter. I was extremely nervous but my anxiety was shared by the men in my class. They told me it had been a long time since they were in a classroom.

It seemed strange now to see homeless men,

begging for money on Tremont street, and living at the shelter.

I continued to see Mary on a weekly basis along with the Psychiatrist who adjusted my medication as needed.

I would regularly meet with Larry at Wendy's and on occasion we would take turns buying lunch. It was the only remaining friend I had from the Factory which they had now began to tear down.

I was finally now on my way.

68

A PLACE OF MY OWN

It was six months before Mary recommended me to move into my own apartment. The welfare office agreed to supplement the cost of the rental.

It was a small studio room located in Dorchester. It was furnished along with a refrigerator, and stove. I was excited about the move and not having to room with twenty men in a barrack like setting. I had even invited Larry to visit me once I was settled in. Larry, at the time, had his own place, which was also in Dorchester. We both enjoyed visiting each other and having supper together.

I continued to work at the training center where I enjoyed a paycheck which I saved towards making the move back to my own family. It felt good to again be useful, helping others rather than obsessing about my own problems. My boss was more than pleased with my work. He was so pleased that he had me teach other courses aside from helping the men get their high school diplomas.

I stopped having nightmares, following my most

traumatic session with Mary in which I related my sons' accident. My life seemed to have turned around after that session. Mary had made a big difference in my life. I would still be homeless and lamenting over my son's death if I had never met Mary.

I'm ready, although anxious to talk to Mary about continuing to move forward.

When I walked through the doors of the shelter, Mary began my therapy, as usual, by asking me how things were going.

"So, tell me Greg, how's the job and your new apartment? That was a big step for you, moving into your own place and working."

"Yes, it was a big step forward but I'm loving it. What a difference it is to have my own place, even thou it's not very big. And the work. It feels so good to be doing something again" I then started to laugh before saying, "And you're right, I didn't forget how to teach."

"Are you making your own meals or eating out?"

"I'm actually learning how to cook believe it or not. I need to save some money. Once in a while Larry and I go to our favorite place, Wendy's for a change in menu."

"Did you ever do any cooking at home?"

I again laughed. "Are you kidding me? No, not at all. Like they say, I couldn't even boil water. Mom did all the cooking in our house."

"So how did you learn to cook?"

I went to see Cookie, the cook at the shelter, who gave me some quick lessons on how to make nourishing but good meals without breaking the bank."

"I am so proud of what you have accomplished Gregory. And in a short period of time. And how's it going at the training center?

"Like I said, terrific. My boss is such a great guy who really take care of his men. I love teaching again and the best part of it all is that I even get a paycheck."

"And what about the nightmare?"

"You won't believe it but there gone Joan. I quickly realized that I was calling Mary by my wife's name and corrected myself. "I mean Mary. Sorry about that. I've been thinking of Joan quite a bit these days and also wondering about my how my daughter Alison was doing? Actually, I was thinking about the whole family? I can't wait to see them all."

"I can see that your family is on your mind especially since the chances of seeing them is becoming a reality with each passing day.

"So, Gregory, what's next for you?"

"I've been thinking, that it might be time to reunite with my family. But I have to tell you Mary I'm scared shitless. Sorry. It just slipped out. I'm hoping they will accept me back."

She said. "What do you think Greg?"

"That's it. I don't know. I need to be prepared for any kind of a response."

"I'm sure you realize, that it's going to be shock for them when they see you. It's been a long time. Remember, like I said before, they don't know whether your alive or dead."

"That's what scares me. How they're going to react to me?"

"I have a feeling that in the end, once they get over the shock of seeing you alive, they will embrace and accept you back."

"I hope so."

"Are they living in the same Place?"

"Yes, I checked it out in the phone directory. Nothing has changed. I was thinking that I might go and see Frank first. I can ask around town, where he's working. He's well known in Arlington. I know I couldn't walk into my house like I had just gone out for the newspaper. That would be too much of a shock to Joan, Alison and myself."

"That might be a good idea. I think he'd be the most receptive of your family. He certainly might help to clear a path for you. Sound like you've given it a lot of thought."

"That's all I've been thinking about these past weeks. What do you think Mary?"

"I think you're ready Gregory. Do you want me to go with you?"

"I'd like that but I think this is something that I have to do myself."

"Your right."

I left Mary's office ready to do it.

69

SAYING GOODBYE

The day finally came a month later when I packed up all my belongings into a trash bag. Not that I had much. I stuffed the money I had made working at the center into my pants pocket. It was now time to say my goodbyes to my friends.

I began by visiting my boss at the training center. The men at the center gave me a going away party. They expressed their thanks for everything I had done for him.

My boss then approached me, "Greg, you'll always have a job at the center, whenever you care to return. You've done good work and the men love you."

"Thank you for giving me a chance. I really appreciated what you've done for me. And I will come back to visit you and the boys. You' will always be a part of my memories. I'll never forget what you've done for me."

I then went over to Larry's place of work, "Margie's Best' to say my goodbyes. Margie's is a small coffee and pastry shop. A place where you can have a nice cup of coffee and enjoy homemade pastries.

I hadn't yet told Larry I was leaving today. When I walked into the shop, he immediately saw the trash bag in my hand. He shook his head as if in disbelief. "You going somewhere Professor?"

He then turned to the owner, Margie and said, "Do you mind if I take a few minutes to talk to my friend?"

She replied. "Not at all. Why don't you get a few coffees and some of the pastries you made this morning? Go sit at one of the tables."

"You're a sweetheart Margie. Thanks."

I sat down at a corner table while Larry got us coffees and some pastry. When he returned to the table I said. "Wow. That looks delicious. Did you, make these things?"

He proudly replied. "Just this morning."

I took a bite into the pastry. "This is terrific. You've come a long way."

"Thanks Professor. So, what's going on with the trash bag?"

"I'm going to make the move home, to be with my family."

I could clearly see the disbelief on his face. "Wow. So, you're really going to do it? Make the big move? Now that takes real guts."

"Yes. It's time. It won't get any easier."

"I have to tell you Greg, I'm going to miss you. I don't know. It's going to be very different around here."

"I feel the same way about you Larry but like I said, its time. I have to tell you Larry, I'm a little nervous. I hope I'm doing the right thing."

"It's the right thing. Now don't forget me. Here's my address, the same one."

"You can bet on it. I won't forget you Larry. And

what about you, have you returned to your mother's place?"

"I'm afraid not. I don't have the same courage as you. Once was enough but in time, I might give it another try. My therapist said, that I need to do it, one more time so as to have some sense of closure."

"That sound like good advice."

"Where you going, to Arlington Professor?"

"Yes. I first need to locate my brother Frank. You know, I've told you about him. He's working on a new development in Arlington Heights."

Larry got out of his chair and hugged me. "Best of luck Professor. I know things will work out for you. You're a good guy."

A small tear rolled down my cheek as I gave my friend a hug.

I walked out of the shop feeling that the door closed on one part of my life that I want to forget. I'm hoping for another door to open that will lead me to my family.

I live in hope.

70

FINDING FRANK

I took the train to Harvard square rehearsing what I might say to my brother when I saw him? *I'm sorry. Hey bro, it's been a long time.*

What do you say when you've deserted the people you love? That's the million-dollar question.

The train stopped at Harvard square and I took the bus all the way to Arlington Heights. I knew that my brother's development was somewhere up the heights but wasn't quite sure of the exact location. Once I got off the bus, I stopped at a local coffee shop, in the hopes that someone would know where the development was.

When I walked into the coffee shop, I took a seat at one of the tables. I was soon approached by a young waitress, a young woman who looked to be about 18 years of age. She was probably a High School Senior looking to make a few dollars. She approached me with a pleasant smile on her face. It was refreshing to see some young people, who were not homeless.

She gave me a menu and asked. "You want coffee?"

"Yes, please."

"And would you like to order a sandwich or something to eat?"

I thought for a minute and said, "Yes."

Aside from the pastry at Larry 's place I really hadn't eaten anything substantial all day and it was now 5:30.

"What can I get you?"

"Why don't you bring me a BLT with mayo."

Before she could turn away, I said. "Excuse me, do you know of a housing development in the area that's being developed by the Byrne Construction Company?"

"Sure, it's about four blocks from her off Parker street. Can't miss it, with all the equipment out in front. Looks like it's going to be a first-class development of big single homes."

I thought to myself, *why not. That's my brother Nothing but the best.*

And then it struck me, that my daughter might be in High School. I wondered if I should ask the waitress if she knows her?

When she returned with my coffee and food. I said, "Thank you. O, one more question. Do you happen to know a young girl by the name of Alison Byrne?

She laughs. "I can see you're not from around her. She's a freshman and a super soccer player. Her uncle owns that construction company. And her Grandmother is something else. She's like the mayor of Arlington. Never misses a game even thou she had a stroke some years ago."

I thanked her and began eating, by taking a sip of my coffee. I paused for a minute and thought to myself, *Thank God mom's alive and well.*

She later returned to my table and said. "Can I get you anything else?"

"No. No. nothing. That will be it."

She then a said, "Why did you ask about Alison? Are you family or something?"

"Yes, a distant friend of the family. I've been away for a long time. Looking to catch up with them."

She then looked down at my trash bag with some skepticism and suspicion and walked away.

I smiled to myself to think that Alison was still playing soccer and it sounds like she' pretty good at it.

I ate my food, left a tip and as I was walking out the door, I noticed that the young girl was whispering something to her manager as I left. I'm sure she was wondering who I really was and what I was up to.

71

THE FIRST MEETING

After I left the coffee shop, I started to walk towards the development site, which was located just where the waitress told me. With every step I took, my stomach was in a state of turmoil. As I got closer to the job site, I began to walk faster until I finally came upon the construction. It was about 6:00 o'clock and I knew Frank would still be working.

One of the workers, who I didn't recognize, was packing up his tools. I approached him and said. "Excuse me. I'm looking for Frank Byrne. Do you know where he is?"

"Sure. I think he's in the trailer, at least that's where he was about 15 minutes ago. Why don't you check." He gave me directions and I quickly reached trailer. I stood in front of the door, reluctant to go inside.

As I was standing there frozen, unable to move a muscle, another worker came by and said. "What can I do for you?"

I suddenly came out of my stupor and said. "I'm here to see Frank.

"He's inside. Go right in."

"Thanks."

I slowly turned the handle of the trailer, fearful of what would happen when Frank saw me.

As I opened the door, I saw Frank busily looking at some housing plans. He was so engrossed in his work that he didn't see me. But the man that was with him, his supervisor, recognized me from the past.

His mouth fell open and he said, "O my God. I don't believe it. Frank."

Frank didn't respond since he was still involved with his work.

"Frank. You have to see this."

Frank was annoyed. "What? Can't you see I'm busy?"

"Frank. Please. Look who walked through the door."

When Frank finally looked up and saw me, I thought he was going to have a heart attack. He was having trouble processing what he saw. "That you Gregory?" I still had a day's growth and my clothes were spoiled.

When he finally realized that it was me, he said to his supervisor, "Sam can you leave us alone?"

"Sure thing." And he left the trailer.

I could see that Frank was still in a state of disbelief. "Am I dreaming? That is, you Gregory?"

I hesitated for a few seconds before saying. "Yes, it's me Frank. Your lost long brother has returned."

He wasn't quite sure what to say, but became angry and began to yell. "Where the hell have you been? We all thought you were dead. What the hell, happened Greg?"

"I've been living on the streets. Homeless for most of the time. I'm sorry Frank. I really am. After my son's death, I just couldn't take it anymore. I had to get away. I just had to."

He continued to show his displeasure. "So, you think you were the only one affected by his death? Well you were not. Dam it all Greg, we were all upset. We needed you to be here, with us"

Frank then began to cry. He came over and gave me hugs.

"Shit Greg, we were beside ourselves. We didn't know what happened to you. Were you run over by a train? Maybe you took your own life. We just didn't know."

"I'm sorry Frank. I didn't mean to cause you all that trouble. I kept blaming myself for Chris' death. I..."

"When you left, Alison went into a depression for weeks. She missed her daddy. She couldn't understand why you left her. Her condition got so bad that Joan needed to get her some professional help. She was so close to you. And Joan, your loving wife, was a mess. And it seemed like mom cried every time your name came up or was mentioned. She really took it bad."

"I am so sorry for causing such problems. I know I screwed up but I was just distraught over losing Chris. I carried around my guilt all those years. I started to drink heavily and eventually ended up homeless. I spent my days living on the streets, in an abandoned factory and sleeping at nights in a homeless shelter. I know that saying I'm sorry doesn't make up for what I did but...I don't know Frank what else to say."

"Okay. I'm sorry for getting so angry but it's time to move on. Tell me, how are you feeling?"

"Physically fine. Mentally, I've been seeing a therapist over the last years who helped me get my act together. If it wasn't for her, I wouldn't be at your doorstep today."

"I'm glad you got some help but you look so thin and gaunt."

"Well, I didn't exactly have the best of diets during those years."

My comments caused Frank to laugh. "I guess you're right.

But it's so good to see you Greg, even thou I'm pissed off and could kick your ass down the street."

"I deserve an ass kicking brother."

"Have you seen the family yet?"

"No, I thought it would be best if I start with you."

"I have to tell you Greg, they're going to be in, for one hell of a surprise. They just never expected to see you again. I hired detectives to look for you. We even checked all the hospitals. You were nowhere to be found. It was frustrating coming up empty handed."

Frank came over and gave me another bear hug. "What do you need brother? Are you hungry? You look like you can use a good meal. I can have one of the guys get something. What Greg what?"

"Frank. Stop it. I'm not hungry. I just want to see my family. What do you think I should do? How should I approach them?"

"Just be honest about what happened and why you left. You can expect them to be angry, furious, that's for sure."

"I know but I deserve it."

"Let me just finish what we're doing and then I'll take you home. Okay?"

I took a deep breath and said, "Okay."

I survived the first round when I saw my brother but I wasn't quite sure what would happen when I would see Joan, my wife and Alison, my daughter.

72

THE FAMILY

$\mathbf{F}$rank quickly finished his work and took me home. I approached the driveway with my heart pounding so fast thst I thought it would burst through my chest.

Frank said, "Joan should be home by now, making supper and Alison will be done with her soccer practice. I think it would be best if I went into the house first and gently break the news to them. What do you think?"

"Yes. I think that would be a good idea."

Frank went into the house, where he told Joan and my daughter, that he had some news about me, that I had returned home and was outside waiting to come in. There was a brief moment of silence, before I heard a lot of yelling and screaming.

The door then flung open and I was greeted by my daughter Alison. She flung her arms around me with tears streaming down her face. She yelled "Daddy. Daddy. You're home. You're home. I missed you so much."

She hugged me so hard that I thought that my bones would crack.

As she hugged me, I could see Joan standing behind her, crying. It was a very emotional moment in our life. "Daddy I'm so glad to see you."

She then proceeded to cover me with kisses. "Daddy. What happened? We thought you were dead."

"I'll tell you the whole story later."

Once my daughter stopped hugging and kissing me Joan just stood there staring at me as if in belief, as if I was a ghost, and not real. Like she was in a dream, not knowing if my presence was a blessing or a nightmare. I didn't know if she wanted to welcome me or kick me out of the house.

I ran to Joan with open arms and embraced her. The words suddenly came gushing out of my mouth. "I am so sorry Joan. So sorry."

She initially stood limp with her hands and arms by her side, not responding to me. She then spoke with her body trembling with anger and rage. "You bastard. You bastard. You fuckin bastard. Why the hell did you do this to us? Why? You just left us without a word?"

She then began pounding her firsts on my chest.

Alison became upset. And started to yell. "Mommy. Mommy don't. Stop it. Stop it. You're hurting daddy."

Frank stepped in and restrained my wife, who was now crying controllable.

"Joan I'm sorry. I didn't mean to do this to you and Alison. I didn't."

She then stood away from me yelling. "You left the house that day and now you return after all those years? Gregory."

"I know. I know. I can never apologize enough for what I did to you and this family."

"But why? Give me one good reason why you left

without even a phone call or a letter. Why? Because of Chris?"

"Yes, because of Chris. I felt so dam guilty that I had to get out of the house. Guilt just drove me away."

"Didn't you think that his death affected me and Alison. That we felt just as bad?"

"I realize that now but at the time I was drowning in my own guilt. I was only thinking of myself. I didn't want to deal with my feelings. I..."

Before I could finish the sentence, Joan interrupted me. "We needed you Greg. You left us alone during the worst time in our lives. We needed you and you left us. I'm so pissed at you. I don't know if I can ever forgive you."

"You have every right to be mad at me. I will try and make it up to you. I love you and Alison so much. While I was away there wasn't a night that I didn't think of you. You were always in my thoughts. Please Joan. Give me a chance. I'm begging you."

Frank stood in the shadows in silence, listening but not saying a word.

"Joan. I only hope that we can start over again. I've been in therapy over the past years which has helped me deal with Chris' death and my own feelings. I'm trying Joan. I really am."

Joan sighed and said. "Come here."

She hugged me and said. "I love you Greg. But if you ever pull that shit again, don't bother coming back home because you won't have a home. Losing Chris was bad enough. I can't go through another loss." She then began to shake me. "Do you hear me Greg? Do you?"

"I do. I can promise you, that whatever happens in our lives, I will stand by your side."

Joan kissed me again and showed a slight smile. "You better. And what about your poor mother? Have you seen her yet?"

"No, I haven't. Frank will be taking me over to the house now.

I'd like to change into some fresh clothes, if you still have them."

Joan laughed. "Clothes? You're lucky I didn't throw them out with the rest of your belongings. They're still hanging in the closet."

"Thanks Joan. Let me get cleaned up and then we can go Frank."

"I'll be here."

After I got cleaned up Frank drove me to mom's home. One more round to go.

73

MOM

As we were driving to mom's house, Frank said. "Greg, let me go in first so that mom won't have a heart attack when she sees you. Everyone will be home, mom, Maria and my son Danny. They'll be wondering why I'm coming home so early. I usually don't finish work until 7:30 or 8:00 pm.

Frank pulled into the driveway with his truck, next to his wife's car. We then went up the walkway and opened the front door.

Once the door was open Danny, his son, began to run towards his father but froze when he saw me, I said, "Yes Danny its's your uncle Gregory."

Mom, who was cooking in the kitchen soon appeared with her walker. "What is all this yelling and shouting about?"

When she saw me, a look of disbelief covered her face. Mom didn't say a word. She blessed herself a few times and finally said, "O my God. Is it you Gregory?"

I replied. "Yes mom, it's me. I'm back and here

to stay for good." I ran over and hugged her fragile body.

Mom's eyes filled with tears as they ran down her wrinkled and tired face. "I can't tell you how good it is to see you Gregory. But why?"

"Mom, I don't want to talk about it now. Maybe another time" I decided to change the subject. "And how are you Maria?"

"Great Greg. Good to have you back. Frank has been lost without you. Have you seen Joan and Alison yet?"

"We just left my house."

Mom continued to absorb the fact that her wayward son was back. "I still can't believe it's you. I just can't. It's been so very long. We were so worried about you."

"I am so sorry for all the worry I put you and the family through. It was stupid."

She then motioned to me. "Come hear my boy. Let mom give you a hug."

I again went by her and she proceeded to kiss and hug her.

I jokingly said, "By the way you hug me mom, it seems like you've gotten stronger."

She laughed. "Well, you know the lady gave me the exercises to do and I do them every day."

Frank said. "She never misses doing her exercises."

"And I hear you still go to the soccer games?"

"I wouldn't miss them. Right Danny?"

Danny laughed. "No, she's always there. She makes the most noise of anyone in the stands."

"That's great Danny. Well, I think I better get back to Joan and Alison. We have a lot to catch up on."

Mom then said. "You, Joan and Alison have to come over the house for Sunday dinner."

"We'd love to mom, once I get settled."

I said my goodbyes and Frank drove me home.

As I got out of Frank's truck, I again thanked my brother who was always there for me. Always.

74

PUTTING THE PIECES
BACK TOGETHER AGAIN

I returned home from mom's house where I talked to Joan and Alison late into the evening. Alison talked about school and her prized soccer trophies. She told me how she spent a lot of time with mom and how she and Danny have become very close. They did everything together from shopping to going to the movies.

Joan talked about her school work but she said it was never the same without me.

When our grandfather struck midnight, Joan said, "Okay Alison, say good night to daddy. You have a long day ahead of you. School and a soccer game at 3:00."

I said, "A soccer game? I'd love to come. Would that be alright princess?"

Alison laughed. "Daddy you haven't called me princess since I was a little girl. I'm a teenager now."

"You'll always be my princess, no matter how old you get."

Alison ran over and hugged me hard and said. "O

daddy, I love you. I am so glad you back home with us. And I'd love you to come to the game. Grandma will be there. It will be fun."

"I'm looking forward to it. More than you can ever imagine. I always knew you'd grow up to be a star soccer player."

She again giggled. "Daddy you're so funny."

"Good night my one and only princess."

"Goodnight Daddy." And she disappeared up onto the staircase.

Once she was upstairs, I just shook my head.

Joan looked at me and said. "What's the matter Greg?"

I still can't believe I'm back home and out of that hell hole. And now Alison is all grown up. She laughs when I call her princess."

"She missed you so much Greg. I won't belabor the point but you hurt her and me so badly. Many a night we both went to bed crying."

"I know that what I did was a stupid thing. I'm ashamed to say I was only thinking of myself and my own feeling. I missed so many precious moments with my family."

Joan responded to me with a sharpness in her voice. "Yes, you did. Dam it all Greg. It hurt." She then paused for a few moments and said. "I'm sorry Greg for being so angry but I was really hurt by your leaving."

"You have right to be angry with me."

"Okay but I think it's now best, if we put all of that behind us and get on with our lives."

"Do you mean it Joan? Do you?"

Joan left her seat and joined me on the sofa, where she put her arms around me and gently kissed me.

"Thank you, Joan. I promise somehow, some way, I'll make it up to you and Alison. I will."

Joan quickly changed the subject. "What was it like being Homeless? I can't image living on the streets."

"How do I describe it? I lived during the day in an abandoned factory until the police and factory owner would no longer allow us to live there. I made friends with three guys. Mac, who was sick and eventually died. His death was very upsetting to me."

Joan's anger then turned to sympathy for what I had experienced. "O Greg. That sounds terrible. How did you ever cope?"

"Not too well. The only way I was able to deal with my homelessness was through Mary the social worker. I tell you Joan, if it were not for her I.. ...I don't know what I would have done."

"And what about your other friends?"

Nick was the other guy I befriended. He was a veteran who suffered from PTSD. He drank too much and was always getting into fights until one day he was murdered."

Joan was appalled by what I said. "Did you say he was murdered?"

"Yes. He got into one fight too many. All these guys including myself had problems. There was a reason why we all ended up homeless. If we had our shit together, we wouldn't have been homeless."

Joan then looked me in the eyes and said. "I feel so badly for everything that you went through."

"It was my own doing Joan. I can't blame anyone else but myself. Then there was one other guy Larry. When I met him, he was 18 yrs. old. He had been on the streets since he was 15."

"Just a kid. So young. Where were his parents.?"

"Parents? His mother was a drunkard and a prostitute who didn't want anything to do with him."

She held my face and said. "I think it's time for you to put that part of your life behind you. You're here now. That's all that matters. Let's start anew."

I kissed her and she kissed me back. "That felt so good Joan."

"I'm exhausted Gregory. You must also be worn out? What say we turn in and call it a night?"

"Sound good to me."

Once in bed, I wrapped my arms around her and began kissing her.

I wanted to make love to her but she pulled away from me.

"Gregory. I can't do this now. You're going to have to give me some

Time and space. I'm sorry. I'm happy that your back....but" She paused but didn't finish the sentence."

"I understand Joan." I turned away from her and went to sleep.

EPILOGUE

The weeks turned into months when I finally was able to get a teaching job with the help of Joan. My daughter Alison who was an A student, continued to play soccer. Mom had us over for dinner every other Sunday. She told Frank, that the housekeeper he hired, could clean the house but the kitchen was off limit to her.

My brother Frank and Maria decided to adopt another boy who was about the same age as Danny.

The pastries that Larry made at the Pastry shop became very well known in the Boston neighborhood. He was also a regular visitor to my home where we enjoy his wonderful desserts. He became known as Uncle Larry to the children.

"So that's my story. Whether you remain homeless or rejoin the human race is up to you. You can do it like Larry and myself did. Take responsibility for your life. There's help here at the shelter if you take advantage of it. Not easy. But with help, you can do it.

One man in the back-row said, "But you had a family to go home to. I don't have anyone."

"Like I said, my friend Larry had no one but he made a life without his family."

But best of all, my wife Joan completely forgave me and our love together, grew stronger than it had ever been."

Then Mary stepped up to the microphone and said. "Thanks Mr., Byrne for coming to the shelter and sharing you story of hope with the men." The men in the room stood up and applauded me.

"Thank you for the opportunity to speak to them Mary. I'll be hanging around if you guys have any questions. I'd be happy to help you in any way I can. But let me end by saying you have a terrific staff here at the shelter. And a wonderful social worker. Take advantage of her. Take advantage of them. Please.."

I finished by saying. "Grab on to hope and hold it tight. Hope can change you"

THE END

CPSIA information can be obtained
at www.ICGtesting.com
Printed in the USA
FFHW021509071019
55429603-61201FF